Ridin' the Five

Brittney'

Thank you so much for getting my books; this one is my favorite. I hope you enjoy the crap out it

Josh

Also by Josh Stricklin

Under the Wolf Tree
The King of Evil
Ridin' the 5

Ridin' the Five

Under the Wolf Tree, Book 2

By

Josh Stricklin

HOLLISTON, MASSACHUSETTS

RIDIN' THE FIVE
Copyright © 2018 by Josh Stricklin

This book is a work of fiction. Names, characters, places and incidents are products of the author's imagination or are used fictiously. Any resemblance to actual events, locations or persons, living or deceased, is entirely coincidental.

Printed and bound in the United States. All rights reserved. No part of this book may be reproduced or transmitted in any form or by any means, electronic or mechanical, including photocopying, recording, or by an information storage and retrieval system—except by a reviewer who may quote brief passages in a review to be printed in a magazine, newspaper, or on the Web—without the express written consent of Silver Leaf Books, LLC.

The Silver Leaf Books logo is a registered trademarks of Silver Leaf Books, LLC.

All Silver Leaf Books characters, character names, and the distinctive likeness thereof are trademarks of Silver Leaf Books, LLC.

Cover Art by Createspace.

First printing July 2018
10 9 8 7 6 5 4 3 2 1

ISBN # 978-1-60975-213-2
ISBN (eBook) # 978-1-60975-214-9
LCCN # 2018939168

Silver Leaf Books, LLC
P.O. Box 6460
Holliston, MA 01746
+1-888-823-6450

Visit our web site at www.SilverLeafBooks.com

For Mamaw and Amanda,
who were tasked with making this book better.
Just imagine what they've been through.

Ridin' the Five

"What is love? Love is playing every game as if it's your last."

- Michael Jordan

1

Welcome to Rose Colline

Long way from home, aren't ya?

Oh yeah, I can tell. Town like this, like Rose Colline? Town's only got a few thousand people. Easy to remember a face. Even easier to spot one that ain't a regular. Passing through or here to stay?

Yeah, that's usually the case.

Me?

Oh, I've been here forever. I love it here. There's something about a small town, you know? You become a bigger part of the life than in a city. Whether you want to or not. That's just the way it pans out. For instance, this bar? This ain't no chain. Someone from Rose Colline has one hundred percent ownership. His name is Chip Anderson. His son's name is too, but everyone just calls him Junior.

Next door, the mechanic is Al Windham. His wife runs the books for him. There are two other mechanics in town, but he's the best, honestly.

All the stores are local like that. Most of them have the owner's name right there in the title. Carlisle Flower Shoppe, Randy's Quick Stop, even Aunt Missy's restaurant is run by Mayor LeBoix's aunt, Missy.

Everything you'll wanna do while you're here is gonna be right there on Beacon: the two-screen movie theater, the bowling alley, they even put the high school down there on the end. There's always something going on in the cafeteria. Since the community center burnt down in '41 they use it for everything. Parties, meetings, live music, I mean everything. They even have lessons where you can learn how to dance. Youngsters teach adults, adults teach youngsters. You'd be hard-pressed to find someone around town that cain't lindy hop.

That's how small town life is, friend. Everybody knows everybody.

Mrs. Jameson and the Michaels family work together with their stores. The Michaels provide discounts to the Jameson Funeral Parlor, so she has nice flowers for those who are bereaved. And she—I'm sure—does something nice for them when they've gone cold.

The Peterson and Moss families run the school. Most of the adults in town learned from the Petersons, but the government got involved and added funds. Now they have a full staff. Basketball team plays every weekend from December to February. I hope you'll come see one while you're here. Even the townspeople without kids in the game show up. And they're good. State champs. Those games will keep you young and make you old all in one quarter. It's like they know they're going to win, but they keep it close for the crowd. Isn't that funny? I know it's crazy to think, but they do. They have a knack for showmanship.

Even further down from the school, just far enough to drown out the cheers on Friday nights, you'll see the houses of the wealthy—Daniel Busby, who's the owner at the car dealership, and Ethan Maxwell, who owns the bank, just to name a couple—and just beyond the edge of our fine little community's reach, there's the Nelson House. I doubt you'll find yourself down there though.

Fair warning, friend. I ain't the only one gonna notice a new face in the crowd.

Where're you from now?

Well, Dallas is a big city. Here you're not gonna blend in so well. Probably never had a body come into your business the way you may experience here. Part of knowing each other the way this town does is completely losing all sense of boundaries. You'll find it strange, I'm sure.

At first people here will even find *you* strange. You're like the one brick house on the block painted black in a line of white wooden houses. It's not that it doesn't belong, it's just different. Different ain't always bad. You'll find that most small towns have very little more to offer than an exit door, especially if you trying to stray from the norm. And we're no different.

But as long as you here, they gonna see you. A small town is an always-watching eye, just out of your periphery. If you're minding your Ps and Qs, won't nobody say a word. You'll be just fine.

I'm so sorry, friend. I'm imposing our town on a passerby. I didn't mean to—

Oh.

Oh, alright then. Nothing better to do. I like that. You see, time moves slower in a small town. Don't be surprised if I talk you to the end of it. Everybody does. Something you may just have to get used to.

Which way did you come from, friend?

Oh, yes. Oh, yes. Texas.

Ah, so you rode the five, didn't you?

Sorry. I don't mean to laugh at you. That's just what we call it.

That's part of our lingo. Just means taking that road you took that brought you here. Don't worry. The longer you stay, the easier it'll be to pick up on that kind of stuff. Just like you'll understand what turns heads and what doesn't.

Soon enough they'll hardly notice you.

Unless you do something out of the ordinary, of course.

So, what brings you here to Rose Colline?

Entertainment, eh?

You wanna open a theater?

You think a town like Rose Colline can support a Broadway theater?

Well, very good luck to you my friend.

I'm actually in the entertainment business myself.

Oh, yes. And not some slapdash naked lady show neither. I'm in the business of *thrills!*

If you keep going down the road you were on when you came into town, you'll see my handiwork. Owner/operator of Johnny D's Carnival Funland, at your service. We weren't always Johnny D's—strategic marketing and face-of-the-franchise moves and all—but one thing never changed, and that's our motto: "You'll never go home unhappy!"

Oh, we've got it all, friend. Lights, bells, whistles, games, prizes, food, and of course, all the rides you've ever heard of.

The carny folk are welcoming, and the food's so good you'll wanna eat it twice.

Between you and me, the rides are so good you'll have to. Ha!

We got'm all, too. One's for the kiddies that go in slow circles, the pirate ship that swings back and forth, and we even have the upside-down rollercoaster. Oh, lot of messes made on the upside-down roller coaster. That's why we keep an extra set of funnel cake and corndog stands nearby.

It's all marketing. That's why I chose this spot. Less than an hour and a half between the Red Stick and New Orleans. So many folks passing through see a little fun in the middle of nowhere, everyone gonna pull into Johnny D's. You cain't help it. It just sucks you in. You come inside and stare down the midway, you'll see everything you ever dreamed of right inside. Everything you ever thought was fun.

There is one thing we don't have though.

I'm sorry, I got caught daydreaming again. Forgive me. What was your question?

Oh, no. No, no, no. I'm not Johnny D. Like I said, marketing and all. We weren't always called Johnny D's. There was a time, for years and years, when Johnny wasn't even around. But since you got a minute, I can tell you how we acquired our prized sideshow barker.

You do?

That's good.

I'm still trying to get a good read on you, friend.

Maybe after, I can tell you about the one thing we still don't have at Johnny D's Carnival Funland. I think you'll get a kick out of it.

But for now, we'll talk about how I found Johnny.

You see, it's only the most travelled souls that can really tell you a story, that can really command your attention. That's the kind of soul we needed for the Funland. You can't just have someone who doesn't know anything about the world. You gotta have someone who's seen the best and worst in people, understands how people think. Someone powerful. Someone you can feel in your presence. That's who Johnny Davis was. Not many people get to hear about the recruiting process. But you. Well there's something about you I don't mind opening up to.

Let me get you another beer.

No, no, no. I insist. I'm paying for your company. Call it a business meeting.

Tax write-off, yeah.

Gary, mind setting up the out-of-towner with another oat soda? Thanks, Gar.

See, small town. Everybody knows everybody.

Whether you like it or not.

Oh, my lord. How rude of me! You stroll into town from across the border, and the first face you see just talks your ears to pieces. Let me be the first to invite you into our quiet Southern town, friend.

Welcome to Rose Colline.

2

Marquee

Jonathan Davis didn't give a damn. Those assholes from high school could say or do whatever they wanted. So what? They were the ones living in the same Nowheresville town ten years later. Johnny was educated. He didn't need the same sophomoric dick-measuring contest for which he always managed to find himself in the position of the ruler.

Trust me, friend. Johnny was only kidding himself. Even gripping the steering wheel of the black, ten-year old Dodge Dart as it rumbled and coughed down route five, Johnny Davis cared very much what those assholes from Nowheresville High thought. Do trust me when I say Nowheresville. Nowheresville was even smaller than Rose Colline if you can believe it. Our quaint little town of Rose Colline is small yes, but the entire town Johnny grew up in didn't equal the student body of our high school. Johnny's class of thirty-five was the biggest the school had ever put out. That was the year they added the second building. Even though not a lot of people ever went on to be anything before or after 1952. And when Johnny left town he never planned to come back. The only reason he even went to the reunion was to go back with his doctoral degree in mechanical engineering in hand and his fancy reach-for-the-stars dream job at his fingertips. Only he never expected Rodney Malone to be there. Rodney never graduated after all.

"Screw those assholes," Johnny announced through gritted teeth to the steering wheel, around which his bony fingers gripped so tightly that his knuckles faded to a pale white. The spiked punch still dripped from his thick black hair onto the sticker nametag, smearing the "Dr. Jonathan Davis" written in marker. He would always be Johnny.

Why did I do all of this? he thought.

I put aside everything for this life. I missed out on friends, relationships, the opportunity for a family. It's been ten goddamn years, and I still get picked on.

You see, he wasn't after praise. He didn't expect them to genuflect at his feet saying, "Oh, great and powerful, Dr. Davis! Please, kind sir. Shower us with your wisdom."

No, no. He wanted to feel normal. He only wanted what we all want from our peers: acceptance. He wanted someone, anyone, to say, "Is that Johnny Davis?" with something like excitement in his voice.

That way Johnny could turn around and say, "Yes! It's me!"

He didn't even wanna correct them. He would wait for them to read his name tag and ask, "Oh, you're a doctor now?"

"Oh, this? Yeah, it's no big deal," he had practiced. But that's not what happened, friend. Not that you couldn't figure that one out on your own. Some things are just worth the theatrics. Wouldn't you agree?

When Johnny walked into the gym of his high school, it was unusually quiet. He had heard it quieter only one other time, after a game, but we'll get to that story later.

There was a banner over the basketball goal that said, "Welcome class of '52!" It covered up the one that said, "1952 basketball state champions 12-1." The one Johnny had helped earn.

Johnny scanned the room. There were about twenty-five faces he recognized from either his 1952 graduating class or one of the surrounding years. He assumed they married into the graduation year. There wasn't a face in the small crowd that he didn't recognize. It was overwhelmingly strange to see the augmented waists and diminished hairlines. A lot of them, most were smokers even back then, were even starting to wrinkle. It was amazing that seeing these older versions of his high school fr—classmates reminded him nothing of how they looked ten years ago. And yet, his mind just accepted that this was how they always looked. He couldn't remember them any other way. He walked forward and spoke to the first group of people he saw.

Johnny spoke quietly, keeping with the apparent theme of the afternoon. "Hey, y'all."

There were two women, and a man from his basketball team. He recognized both of the women, but only remembered the name of one, Victoria Barlow. The man was Gerald Herrin. Johnathan checked the name tags hoping to find the missing name, but the woman's red hair fell over the sticker. He did notice, however, that Victoria's last name was no longer Barlow.

"Hey, Johnny," Gerald said, reaching for a strong handshake and getting one. Johnny thought Gerald was trying to rearrange his knuckles.

"Where have you been? I don't think I've seen you since high school."

"Oh, you know. Living the dream."

"I do," Gerald said, laughing. "I do. You remember Victoria? We got married in fifty-three. And Janet Harsgrove."

"Myers," Janet interrupted. Her voice stabbed the air.

"Sorry, Janet. I forgot."

"Oh, no. Don't be sorry. Because this time last year I was still Janet Harsgrove. At this same goddamn event for him."

"I'm sorry to hear that," Johnny told her.

"He's shit. Don't be." Janet sipped her wine. "You're clearly doing well, *doctor*."

"Oh, yeah. Graduated in sixty with my doctorate."

"Southern?" Janet slurred.

"LSU actually."

"It's good to see some of us have reasons to gloat."

"Oh, I didn't mean to gloat or anything. Just catching up. Isn't that why we came here?"

"What?" Janet snapped. "To rub your success in our faces?"

"That's not what he's doing, Janet," Victoria spoke up

with a slur of her own. She turned to Johnny. "She's just bitter about the divorce. She's not jealous that you're doing better than us."

"*Bitter?*"

"I'm not necessarily doing better than y'all. I still don't even have the job I want."

"I'd hope you're doing better than us," Victoria said. "You went to college. If you don't even have a job, then why'd you go to college?"

"I do have a job, I just—"

"Hey, Johnny!"

Johnny graciously turned to the voice without excusing himself from the conversation.

The first friendly face was his cousin, Matt. He didn't think he'd even spoken to Matt in as many years as he had the rest of them. What had he walked into? This gym was some sort of portal to the past. Matt shook his hand.

"Janet Myers seems like a wreck," Johnny told him.

"Oh yeah, she caught her husband in bed with a student. Or on a desk I guess is the right way to think about it. He's in the jailhouse now."

"She's taking it well."

"Yeah." Matt stood there looking for something else to say. The gym was quiet enough that the ticking could be heard between sobs from Janet Myers. "So, *Doctor* Jonathan now, huh? That's cool, man."

"They seem to think so, too."

"Yeah." Matt said.

Johnny started to say something and Matt spoke at the

same time. Johnny awkwardly laughed. "No, you go ahead."

"Nah, you go."

"I was honestly just going to say that it was tough. Getting my degree."

"Oh, yeah," Matt said. He cleared his throat loudly. "You may be the only one here who actually went to college."

"That can't be true."

"No, I think you're it. Everyone else either went to work for the state or construction somewhere. Lot of roads coming up everywhere. The five might even get shut down one day."

For some unexplainable reason, Johnny suddenly felt bad, guilty for doing better than the rest of them. Why should he have to feel bad for actually trying?

"So what kind of doctor are you?"

"Mechanical engineering."

"So like machines?"

"Yeah, sure."

"Oh, I see. So not like a real doctor?"

"I'm a real doctor."

"But not like a person doctor."

"I'm a scientist." Johnny just wanted his cousin to understand what he was saying, but the look on Matt's face told Johnny that that would never happen. "But yes. Like a machine doctor. I operate on them and everything."

The reality that all of this was a mistake quickly settled into Johnny. All he felt was a powerful need to leave. Despite how much he always loved being in the gym, this feeling felt familiar to him.

Johnny's shirt constricted around his chest and neck.

"Hey, I'm going to step outside a minute," Johnny told Matt.

"Sure thing. Come back quick. There's some people you gotta meet."

"Right, right. I'll be right back," Johnny said, knowing he had met everyone here a long time ago. He made for the exits.

As he broke away, the embarrassment drained. He focused on the door, so much so that he didn't see the human wall until he crashed into it, biting his lip. He rebounded and nearly fell to the ground. His hands checked for blood, but came away clean. The horror inside magnified when he heard that horrible donkey-bray laugh from Rodney Malone.

"Johnny Davis, huh? I thought that was you."

"Hey, Rod."

"*Rod?*" he shouted. He was even wider than in high school, and his hair was practically gone. Johnny couldn't help but notice that Rodney hadn't come here alone. He wondered if Brett and Eli were also married. In high school they did everything he did. Johnny was certain now that nothing ever changed. "Ain't nobody called me Rod since high school. Hey, what'd we call *you* in high school?" The woman spurring him on laughed loudly. Johnny didn't recognize her.

"I don't know, Rodney," Johnny said, eyeing the door.

He couldn't help but assume that Rodney still worked for his dad's carpentry business. He may even be the manager at this point.

"No, sure ya do. It was Little Bitch, right?"

"I don't think that was me, Rodney," Johnny said, but he knew it was. He checked his lip and tried to push past Rodney. Rodney gripped his arm.

"Hey, where you headed, Johnny?" He caught a glimpse of the nametag on Johnny's shirt. His mouth split in an even wider smile, "*Oh,* I'm sorry. *Doctor* Jonathan Davis. Well, excuse me."

"It's fine. Excuse me." Johnny tried to walk around, but Rodney, ample but surprisingly light on his feet, stepped in front of him, and spun him by his shoulder.

"Where you going? I'm just kidding. What? You come back as some faggy doctor and cain't take a joke all'a sudden?"

"No, I just need to step outside for a minute."

Rodney started forward, forcing Johnny to step backward. "Where you gotta go in such a hurry? Ain't nothin' outside. Everything's in here, and we haven't even started."

Everyone was looking at them then. They always were. Especially in that gym. That was something you had to get used to when it came to dealing with Rodney. There was always a crowd. Johnny wondered what Rodney could accomplish if he'd use that crowd control skill for good. Johnny was too focused on the eyes watching him to notice the one pair that wasn't: Rodney's. That particular pair of eyes was looking over Johnny's shoulder, to someone standing behind him. Johnny would've turned to look if his desire to leave wasn't stronger than the feeling that someone was waiting behind him.

"Just let me go outside, man. I'm not bothering you." Johnny felt his feet hit something, and he stopped.

"I miss this, little bitch," Rodney said. "Just like old times."

Rodney slammed his palms into Johnny's chest, sending him backwards over Brett who was crouching behind him. Johnny fell over and knocked into the table.

"Oops!" Eli shouted in feigned surprise.

The punch fell on Johnny like Niagara. Most of the people who were looking were now laughing, including Rodney, with his horse teeth and donkey-bray laugh.

"Just like high school, Rodney," a voice said.

Johnny stormed out of the gym and got back on the five headed back to Baton Rogue, never looking back down that dirt road under the feet of Nowheresville. Johnny boiled with anger.

And that's part of being in a small town. Weakness and strength are physical. There's that sort of tacit agreement of, "Oh they didn't mean anything by it," or "Well, that's just boys being boys," if you know what I mean.

There's a butt to every joke, and in a small town there aren't enough butts to go around.

There's a very interesting thing that happens to people in a place like Nowheresville. Places like these. It's a sad thing really. The ride to the top of the food chain is a short one. People find solace in such small amounts of power. They latch onto it and are so afraid to lose it that they never do anything that would cause their power to shift. They never do anything to make themselves more powerful for fear of losing it all. And heaven forbid someone challenge what they have. Nothing more, nothing less. Just what they already have. Most people find their pinnacle in high school. If your level of popularity is already so high, why strive for more? Why move to some far away college where people don't even know who you are? Especially when you have a nice, easy job right here, waiting for you. Now that we understand the very limited mindset of Rodney Malone, Brett Hankins, and Eli Barns, I suppose there's no more to mention of them for now. They'll be back though. Trust me, they got nowhere to go, friend. But I can tell you're interested.

You ain't drank a sip of that new beer. I don't mean to call you out or nothing I'm used to reading people. Force of habit.

Things weren't always bad in Nowheresville for Johnny. A long, long time ago he was quite a normal kid. He had a bike he loved, read comic books, and got up every Saturday morning to watch the all day marathon at the Marquee Theater down the road. He had a couple friends he palled around with, but never really had a girlfriend. There was a limited pool to select from, of course I don't have to tell you, most of the young women wanted time with Rodney and his cronies, and most of them got it. There was one who never got it, and she never wanted any. Her name was Harriet. Johnny never knew if his unflinching affection for her stemmed from her obvious disgust of Rodney Malone, or her brilliant white smile.

Johnny wasn't fooling anybody. Harriet was beautiful in every way. Her body was thin with infinitely long legs. Her hair fell just past her shoulders and always curled at the ends in big black rings. Her pale skin made her pink lipstick explode with color. That was the only make up she wore. You could see the few freckles on her nose and cheeks. Johnny loved her glasses most of all. No one ever liked the girls with glasses, but Johnny had'm too. It was a match made in heaven. The only chink in that plan was that she never came back after junior year. And believe it or not that was the year Johnny was going to ask her to the prom. It just never worked out. No one knew where she went. At times, it seemed like no one even remembered her. Nobody said a word when she left.

Luckily for me, I have a gift for finding lost people. It's just like magic. After all, that's what us folk in the entertainment business are selling. Magic. An escape. That's what I gave Johnny. An escape. Because you see, as he sat there fuming over what happened, ready to break the wheel right off the dashboard, he was trapped. As he stared at that pink and purple horizon at the end of his vision, he wondered how he managed to paint himself into such a dark corner. There was no way out for him. Except through me. I let his anger breathe. Everyone deserves to let the anger abate. This would be the last time he would ever be angry.

"It's always him," he said in the heat he had created in the black Dodge Dart. "It's always Rodney." When his tears stung his eyes, that's when I knew it would turn to sadness.

And that's where Harriet came in.

"It's okay, honey," a voice smooth like jazz soothed his ear. She slid her hand over one shoulder to the nape of his neck. It only took an instant to get to him. The thought that he should be alone in the car almost finished forming before it was gone. He looked over to Harriet. Her white smile seemed to glow in the fading sunlight. Her lips were as pink as the clouds. Her black dress sparkled as though every star in the galaxy had been woven into its fabric. The slit in the side reached halfway up her thigh. Johnny was literally stunned.

The corners of her mouth turned up, and Harriet said, "Some people never do anything after high school." She waited for realization to wash over him.

Slowly, it came to him. They were married, but for how long he couldn't remember. Were they married in college? Did they get together at the Senior prom like he had planned? When was their anniversary? The specifics were too far out of reach. There was something he could grasp onto for their life. He was head-over-heels for this woman, who had mysteriously appeared in his car.

"Harriet," the name eased past his lips. Something inside him fought, rejected, this reality. Something told him this wasn't right. The smell sealed it. That smell she had always carried with her, peppermint and bubblegum. He never understood why she smelled that way, but that smell was engraved in every memory of her. That smell brought him all the way back to high school. It was just like all those times he had passed her in the hall, or waited on her at the drive-thru, or walked by her at the games. It was the same peppermint and bubblegum smell after all these years. Finally, Harriet was able to take hold. "Thanks, honey," Johnny said as the anger cooled. "I just don't understand how someone can act like that. A thirty-year-old acting like a teenager."

"I know, but look at all you've done. All he hasn't done. You've done all these great things, and I'll bet you he's never even left Louisiana. We've been to New York City. The Big Apple. Besides." She leaned in and kissed his cheek. "Things are about to change for you." She smiled wide at him.

"Thank you," he said and smiled right back.

She returned to her place in the passenger seat of the car, and this time she took his hand with her. The temperature in the car cooled. Johnny was at ease.

"Oh, honey! Let's go." Harriet said.

"Where?"

She pointed to a billboard for Dandy D's Carnival Funland. The billboard was colorful and vibrant. There was a sideshow barker gesturing beneath a marquee entrance. Inside, there were laughing families and children riding rides.

"A carnival?"

"I think it's more of a theme park," Harriet explained.

"Carnivals move around, don't they?"

"I think it's just a catchy name," Harriet explained. "I can't imagine a billboard like that for a temporary event. What do you say, can we go?"

Johnny couldn't help but smile. "Of course. We wouldn't

be coming home yet anyway."

"Oh, wonderful!" Harriet exclaimed, giggling.

The car pulled off the five and onto a gravel road. The wheel shook his hands. The rumble under the tires drowned out any noise in the cab. The road leading from the highway to the carnival was lined with trees. Also part of the magic. Lull them with boring trees and atmosphere for a mile or two, then *bam!* Excitement out of nowhere! Johnny turned the corner and much the same way a stage curtain will do, the tree line parted before him, revealing Dandy D's Carnival Funland.

"Honey, look!" Harriet said with excitement in her voice. "Look at all the lights!"

The lights were so flashy and bright that they reflected on his face inside the car. A rush of joy surged through him. That's my job, you know. Give people fun. Hook'm in the parking lot and reel'm in. It wasn't the lights that hooked Johnny though. It wasn't the laughter or the screams from the thrill rides either. It was the smell of corn dogs that took him back to high school. Back to his first job.

It was a real shitsplat near the police station that served burgers, fries, chicken tenders, and corn dogs. Shakes were the house specialty. They made a mean strawberry shake. There were picnic benches outside so the customers had a place to sit. They filled up fast, too.

On the Fourth of July the parking lot filled to dangerous capacity. People had to see those fireworks. The place was called Phil's drive-through. It was barely more than a concession stand honestly. Just a white two-room building. The front was the kitchen; the back was the stockroom. The customers walked up to the window, waited for the food and left. Simple. Perfect job for Johnny to get his feet wet every day after basketball practice. He went from cook to cashier to assistant manager in the amount of time it took to go from practice squad to sixth man to starter. He didn't care for the work, and he definitely didn't care when a customer yelled at him for not getting enough mayonnaise on the burger.

The reason he stayed was for Harriet. Every day after cheerleading practice the squad and a few football players came to hang out on the tables before the evening rush. More often than not, she would be the only cheerleader without a football player.

They were sophomores the first time he saw her. He recognized her from school where they only passed each other in the hallway.

Johnny had classes at the far end of the building. No one ever said so, but that was where the smarter kids had class. Only eight kids in the entire school had classes down there, and Harriet wasn't one of them. Most of them were socially awkward. So when Johnny took the orders of the cheerleaders and their boyfriends, it was just another chance to be near her. Those afternoons peering through that window, waiting for practice to be over, were the days he loved. Those were the days when she would come. The cheerleaders went to the football games and basketball games. Small town. Only one squad. They were even the batgirls for the baseball team over the summer. They did it all.

When basketball season came around, that's when they'd really meet. He'd score the game-winning three-point shot, and they fall for each other. Written in the stars. Then they'd have a token basketball player in their group of footballers.

Different. But not too different.

Just like Johnny.

When he took her order, the smell of her gum and peppermint tickled his nose, making him clumsy. That never happened with anyone else. Maybe it was the temporary interruption from the meat grease and chili smell, but I think we both know that's not why he noticed the way she smelled. Puppy love is a powerful emotion. He saw every single freckle on her face. The detail in the color of her eyes. The shape of her nose. The way her cheerleading uniform covered everything but that little glimpse of her collarbone. He watched every detail every time he took her order, and every time it amazed him. Johnny was always too nervous to say much more than inquiring of her ketchup preference.

Chicken tender basket and a chocolate shake, and she never gained a pound.

Unheard of.

Teenagers. Excuse my rolling eyes.

It only took a week before he learned her order exactly the way she liked it. No salt on the fries, extra salt on the chicken. "When you finish shaking the shake, could you drizzle some chocolate over the top?"

Sometimes she got a burger, but she always got a shake. Eventually, she stopped asking when Johnny took her order.

She didn't know his name, but she trusted him with the specifics of her milk, ice cream, and chocolate syrup. That was one point of pride he took away from the job.

And as he drove up to Dandy D's Carnival Funland, he couldn't escape the nostalgia that the smell of corn dogs carried with it.

The sun had all but set, creating a layer of orange like embers keeping the cotton candy-colored sky warm. The light from the rides and concession stands shown on Harriet's face as brightly as her smile. Johnny had never seen her so happy.

"Come on," he said. "Let's have some fun."

He left the car to open her door. Something happened when he did. Something he didn't notice. No longer soaked to the gills with pink punch, Johnny wore a pair of clean black slacks. His shirt was a clean pressed white button up, and the sleeves were short. The smeared nametag wasn't even a memory. But most importantly, he was dry. But he was always dry. That's what he would've told you if you asked him.

Johnny walked around the front of the car, unable to look away from the lights and the rides. The entire time, Harriet watched in amazement as the carnival sight danced across her view. Johnny opened the door and offered her his arm. She took it, grinning.

"Why, thank you, Dr. Davis," she said. She was different now, too. Instead of her hair falling to her shoulders in natural, effortless curls, it now dangled behind her in a ponytail. The dress, which reminded him of the sparkle in her eyes, had been replaced with a bright yellow sundress. For the second time in only moments, she was the most beautiful he had ever seen her. They walked toward the marquee entrance. "Johnny, it's wonderful!"

"Shall we?" Johnny motioned toward the gravel walkway leading to the marquee.

"Yes, we shall." Harriet led him up the path, practically skipping. Johnny struggled to keep up, but he made it right by her side. That's her secret. Her excitement creates more excitement.

The marquee was and is an enormous white metal construction. There are blue lights surrounding the sign that flicker in rhythm that look like movement around the words.

Dandy D's Carnival Funland!

It was painted across the top of the sign. And underneath, our slogan: You'll never go home…unhappy!

Johnny noticed a small red drop fall from the sign.

They could hear the voice of our temporary barker. Back then, we were trying it out. Having stand-ins until we found the one.

I remember that day we had Marty at the front. You always remember that one right before the best one. He's a resident mascot. Depending on the impending holiday he could be a bunny, or an elf, or what have you.

On that day, nothing important was close, so he was wearing makeup that looked like a dirty clown. His lazily-applied face paint was smeared and peeling. On his wildly oversized onesie there were blue, green, and orange polka dots along with some tiny red stains. The suit was topped with three pom-pom puffball buttons as red as his wig. His voice was cheerful, and there were plenty of folks gathered around listening. It just didn't fit.

Not quite.

With this position, you don't want someone who's simply interesting. The barker is the first person to interact with the customers. The representation of the company. The face of the franchise. Silly will not do. You need intrigue.

Mystery.

This person absolutely must command your attention and sell you just enough to make you famished for whatever delectable goodies wait on the other side. It was time for Johnny to come home.

"Welcome!" Marty exclaimed. His voice oozed out like slime. His mouth crooked up on one side. "Admission for two?"

Johnny and Harriet cheerfully laughed, hand-in-hand.

"Well," the clown said. "I can't charge a couple of lovers as happy as you."

"Oh, we wouldn't ask you to do that," Harriet told the clown.

"We don't mind paying to get in."

"No, you two go on in."

"Thank you," Johnny said, smiling.

"Come on, honey." Harriet pulled Johnny through the entrance.

There's something different about being outside the Funland looking in, and being inside the fun land. It's almost as though passing through the marquee makes everything…brighter. It has to. Otherwise, it would be a sad, somber affair.

In this new world where pinks are pinker and blues are bluer, Johnny saw it all. All the rides and buildings and stands, all the way up to midway to the haunted house. To me. With the wide, empty space across the way, it waited broad and eerie. All alone. The windows were boarded up, creating the appearance of eyes, and the door was a long screaming mouth.

In the 1800s, the mansion belonged to a plantation owner. After things changed, the owner retired and moved to Florida. He left it run down and falling apart. Then I happened to stumble upon it in the overgrown field, applied the thin layer of black paint and opened for business. I built outward from there. Everything leads to the haunted house. I liked it standing alone. I thought it added to the mystery. A sort of "even the rides don't wanna get near it" type of vibe.

Johnny didn't even see the vacant space though. He only saw cheerful patrons walking across his vision. The families hopped from rides to games to stands, every which-a-way. Johnny was secretly jealous of them. The families. But he and Harriet were still young. Kids are still more than possible.

"What do you wanna do first?" Johnny asked. "Food or a game?"

"You think you can still shoot?" she grinned, motioning to the basketball hoop game.

"That a challenge, my lady?"

"Oh, yes. But first, let's get some ice cream." Harriet

nudged him toward the ice cream trailer.

They waited at the end of a four-person line. At the head of the line, a dad handed his son, who was probably no more than five or six, an ice cream cone. As the dad turned back for his own treat, the son took no more than three steps in Johnny's direction before tripping over his own feet like kids tend to do.

The ice cream flew another two feet toward Johnny before splattering on the dirt path with a quiet, muffled *pff*. The son's face became a caricature of each of the five stages of grief. Before hitting a full on hissy fit, one of my mascots stepped in to save the day. He was a mime. Let me tell ya, if you'd think it's easy to soothe a lost ice cream-fueled tantrum, you may have damage in the attic. But I only acquire the best.

Johnny watched the son's face threaten to turn red. The dirty blob of sugary treat lay dead center between himself and the boy. An unusual thought came to him. It was something so unlike Johnny that he was almost ashamed that he thought it.

Stop being a fucking pussy.

Why did he think that? Johnny certainly didn't know. But suddenly he did. He had been that kid twenty-five or so years before. We've been around a long time. He was here at this Carnival Funland, standing in this exact line. It wasn't deja vu he felt. That's too weak of a feeling. This was a memory. One he had forgotten.

He stood here with his own dad and his mother, which meant he couldn't have been more than six. "Mama,

Mama" he could hear himself saying. His hand went up to pull on his mother's skirt the way it had back then. "Mama! I want a chocolate!"

The memory was so vivid that the sight of his mother the way she looked back then tightened his chest and brought a tear to his eye.

"I know, sweetie," the young and vibrant Edie Davis told her son. She had just had her hair done in long blonde curls. She didn't want anything ruining the feeling of the fresh new haircut. "Daddy's going to get some for all of us."

Merle looked back over his shoulder. The grimace on his face was visible at any angle. Johnny was a little momma's boy.

More than four years and still not off the tit. His momma's gone make him a queer.

There were already food stains on Merle's white sleeveless shirt. The black stains on his pants and hands remained the cornerstone of his fashion since before he was a teenager. Back then they didn't call them teenagers. They were just small adults who didn't have to work for as much money. He had been in and out of factories ever since.

"I'm going to get chocolate, momma!"

As the family of three moved closer to the window, Merle grew more and more annoyed with his son's voice. He looked back over his shoulder again. Edie could see that he was starting to boil over. She knew that it wouldn't be long before everyone else saw it too.

People wouldn't have thought they were together: Edie with her clean white skirt, holding her three year old, and

Merle, greasy and standing two feet in front of them at all times. Edie didn't love those stains; they made her feel dirty. What she loved about him was his big mechanic's arms. She loved having them wrapped around her, even if she didn't know what they were capable of when he lost his temper. All the time they had been together, he had never hurt her. Not really. Nothing bad.

"I wanna chocolate, momma!"

Edie saw that Merle was literally turning red with anger. She scooped up little Johnny into her arms and whispered to him. "I know you do, sweetie. But we need to keep it a secret."

"How come?"

"Well, if the nice ice cream man hears that you want chocolate, he may go ahead and whip up your cone and lay it to the side."

"Yeah!"

"Oh no, that's not good. Because then it will melt. Then you'll have to drink it all up like cold soup. And we can't have that, can we?"

"Huh uh," Johnny admitted with a frown.

"That's right," Edie assured him. "So let's just keep it between you and me. We'll *surprise* the nice man, sound good?"

"Surprise. Yeah!"

Johnny fell quiet.

Merle faced forward. Edie took this to mean that the storm was calming. Then the line moved forward, and Merle leaned on the counter. "A chocolate and a vanilla."

"Cones?"

"Yeah."

"Alrighty, sir," the ice cream man said. "Would you care for a soda?"

"There ain't no beer in there, is it?"

The ice cream man grinned at Merle.

"Why you eyeballin' me?"

"Tell you what," the ice cream man whispered. He made sure no one was listening, but mostly it was all an act. It's all an act. "I'm not supposed to do this, but it's a dreadfully hot day. If you manage to get alone today, come back and see me. Knock on the door." The ice cream man jerked his head to the back of the truck. He would've topped it off with a casual you-don't-tell-and-I-won't-tell wink, but even the ice cream man knew that'd be too much over the line. Instead he left their agreement the way it was. He reached outside of Merle's view and brought back a chocolate cone and a vanilla cone. Merle took them, looking sideways at the grinning ice cream man.

"I'll be back," Merle said. He turned around and handed Edie both of the cones. She put little Johnny back on the ground and took the cones from Merle.

"Chocolate," Johnny said, his eyes wide and bright with blind amazement at the sugary scoop atop the waffle cone. It was the single greatest sight of his life.

"Chocolate," Edie agreed. She slowly lowered the chocolate cone. Johnny bounced on his feet. "Now be careful. I don't want you to drop it."

"I won't. I won't," Little Johnny assured her. He grabbed

the cone with both hands. With Edie in front of him and Merle behind him, Johnny happily walked toward the carousel. He was able to taste the chocolate only once before he bumped into his mother, accidentally shoving the cone into his own face. He was so shocked that he couldn't breathe.

Edie didn't react at first. Merle's hands often swiped at her backside even in public. This was lighter though, more gentle than him. She brushed down the back of her skirt, if for no other reason than to smooth out any wrinkles. Her hand came away sticky and brown. She couldn't process what had happened until little Johnny began crying.

Instinctively Edie spun around to her child. His face was covered with wet, sticky goo. She didn't have any paper towels, so without a moment's consideration Edie toweled his face with her skirt. "Shhh, sweetie. It's okay."

"My ice cream!" Johnny screamed.

Edie frantically shushed him and cleaned his face. She looked up to Merle who was red and fuming. "It's okay, baby," she told Johnny. "Here, honey, just eat mine. It'll be fine."

"It's not chocolate though!" Johnny yelled

"Edie," Merle interrupted. He crossed his arms over his barrel chest. "Shut him up. You're making a scene. Don't make me do it."

"Honey, listen to me. Daddy's getting mad."

"My chocolate," Johnny whined.

"Shut him up, I said."

Edie panicked. Tears formed in her eyes. "Sweetie, please." She licked the piece of her skirt she was using to clean Johnny's face. Nothing she did was helping.

Merle stomped forward and pushed Edie out of the way. He yanked Johnny around by his sticky arm. "Boy, you stop being a fucking pussy. You messed up. Now stop crying about it."

His anger scared Johnny, and the crying continued.

Merle slapped him in the mouth.

"Merle!" Edie screamed.

"Shut up! If you was doing what you was supposed to, I wouldn't have had to get involved. Now, look at me, boy. You quit that sissy crying, or you won't ever get another fucking thing as long as you live. You hear me?"

Johnny's breath hitched violently as he forced composure. "Y-y-yes, s-sir."

Merle pushed him backward into Edie's arms. "You making that boy queer, Edie."

Edie knelt. "I'm sorry, honey. You have to listen to me when I tell you not to cry."

Johnny pouted and sniffled, but he stopped crying. He did that for her. The embrace of his mother got rid of all the bad things. Even at three years old, he knew that if he would stop crying, his father would leave him alone. So that's what he did. No more tears.

Edie stood from her crouch, watching Merle hammer with his fist on the back door of the ice cream truck. Johnny huddled to her side like a cub. There were no rides that day. Only beer and waiting for dad to finish his beer and get them family back on the five and home.

Johnny couldn't pinpoint why such a vivid thought came

to him. It was so powerful that he didn't realize he was gripping Harriet's dress as tightly as he had his mother's all those years ago. Harriet didn't show any sign that she noticed, but she knew exactly what was playing in his mind.

"I think I want a cup of strawberry," she said. "What kind do you want?"

Johnny paused. He was suddenly aware that in his entire adult life, he had never eaten chocolate ice cream. He couldn't remember ever trying it, other than when he was three anyway. "I think I want to try a chocolate scoop. But in a cone."

"A cone? You never have a cone."

"Yeah, I know. I guess I just want to try something new."

When it was their turn to step up to the window, Harriet raised her excitement again.

"Good day, sir," she said. "I'll have a cup of strawberry, and my husband would like a cone with chocolate, please."

The preparation was immediate. The ice cream man reached just beyond where Johnny and Harriet could see without hesitation. He handed Harriet her cup and Johnny his cone.

There's no way he was that fast, Johnny thought.

"And there we are, folks," the ice cream man told them. It seemed their cheerfulness was contagious.

"That was very quick," Johnny praised. "How much do we owe ya?"

"That'll be a…well look at you two. Giddy as children. How long you been together?"

"Well," Harriet said, laughing. She slid her hand into Johnny's. "I guess forever."

"Get a load of that. I can't, in good faith, charge you for something so trivial as ice cream. It's on the house. Well, truck."

"Really?" Johnny said. His smile was as inextinguishable as Harriet's. "Why not?"

"Well, just look how happy you two are. Those grins are payment enough."

"Are you joking?" Harriet asked.

"Of course not! Does a body good to see happy faces. You two go on now," the ice cream man winked. "Have fun out there."

"Well, thank you, sir." Johnny said. Harriet was already pulling him in another direction.

"Come on, big shot. You have to win a Teddy bear for me."

"Do you think that's strange?" Johnny asked. He bit a large chunk of the ice cream off the cone. The taste was so overwhelming he stopped walking. He took another smaller taste and nearly gasped. "Oh my God, this is the best ice cream I've ever had."

"I know, isn't it?" Harriet was busy with her own ice cream. "It's delicious."

"This place is all-around better than any other carnival or fair or whatever this is than I've ever been to," Johnny told her. His mouth was full of ice cream and waffle cone. He had wolfed it down in three tries. Even though it was gone, the taste stayed with him. "The smell is great. The ice cream is incredible. We haven't paid for anything yet."

Harriet laughed. "You haven't yet. You're going to pay for it if I don't get a prize." Harriet winked at him as she ate another spoonful of vanilla. He put his arm around her waist and the two walked together toward the basketball hoop game.

They could hear the carney before ever getting a good view of the game. They heard other barkers at closer stands, but for some reason, Johnny could pick out the words of the basketball hoop carney better than all of them. Like he was calling to Johnny, and all the others were only there for show.

"Step up! Step up! I got your prizes right here. Two pennies gets you four shots, and four gets you ten. Step up and win yourself the giant teddy bear. You, sir!" The carney pointed down the midway to Johnny. He wore a clean, tailored, three-piece suit as white as his teeth. His hair was long—still not a fashion I'm fond of—but slicked back, which helps his look. The carney smelled like tobacco and his voice was thunderous. He was sitting on a stool with a basketball under one foot. Johnny pointed back to himself. "Yes, you. White shirt. Don't you wanna win that sweet young lady a prize?"

"Absolutely, that's why we're here after all. How many do I have to make for the big black and brown one up there?" Johnny pointed to the largest bear the carney had to offer.

"Oh! We got ourselves a competitor, do we?" the carney said. Now he wore a crisp, and clean blue and white striped suit with a matching hat.

"Oh I think so, Larry," the carney's wiry little helper said. He was in a tank top and dirty jeans, much like Merle's typical "going out" attire. Johnny immediately hated him, not knowing that his clothes were the only reason why.

"I see that, Percy," Larry said. "I tell you what, usually no one gets that one. But I don't wanna embarrass you in front of your wife." Larry winked at Harriet, who rolled her eyes. It was all pretend, of course.

"That's very funny. How many?"

"Three," Larry said. He stood up, a good six feet, and six inches tall. He used his hands to flatten any potential wrinkles. "But I'm on defense."

Johnny laughed, "What? Are you going to stay back there?"

"Unless you think you can make it three times in a row from far enough away that me standing here won't matter." Larry passed Johnny a ball. It wasn't an aggressive toss, but in a game it wouldn't have gotten stole. Johnny caught it.

"That's back by that trash can, just so you know," Percy said, and Johnny ignored.

"Lucky for me this was the one thing I was good at back in high school," Johnny explained. He dribbled the ball once, and he could feel it come to him, like they say riding a bike will do for you. He dribbled again. He could almost hear the echo in the empty gym.

"Lucky for me, you hadn't been in high school for what? Six years?"

"Ten."

"Pah!" Larry snorted with laughter alongside Percy. "You done messed up. I tell you what, you pay for one ball, you can shoot 'til ya miss. You ain't going home with that bear though. I tell ya that."

"What's that, a penny?"

"A penny," Larry grinned sideways. He jangled a cup that was hiding behind the barrier between customer and carney. "Shoot 'til ya miss."

Johnny reached into his pocket, and retrieved a penny.

He offered the coin to Larry, but Larry didn't take it.

"Go on back," Larry said. His grin widened.

"Back here?" Johnny said walking backwards to the surprisingly clean garbage barrel.

"That'll do," Larry told him.

Johnny took one more step back so that he would be behind the can. Harriet watched him, reminded of why she fell in love with him all those years ago.

Johnny squared his shoulders and took a deep breath as he honed in on the rim. His focus was paramount. He raised the ball over his head and without leaving his feet, he tossed the ball high into the air. A shadow fell across Larry's face as it passed through the overhead lighting on its way to the net. Not the rim. Not the background. The ball touched nothing but net.

"That's that old pepper," Larry said. He was smiling like a fool. "Am I 'bout to lose the biggest prize I got?"

"Yeah," Harriet said. "Yeah, I think so."

Johnny walked up to Larry to retrieve the ball. "Sure I can't pay you for the other ones?"

"You got two more," Larry smirked.

"Suit yourself," Johnny said. He dribbled the ball between each hand. Right to left. Left to right. Quicker and quicker. He could feel the sixteen-year-old version of himself stirring. He even tried a fake, expecting to fall flat on his face. He dribbled the ball again, but before it rose more than a foot off the ground, Johnny planted his foot, stopped the ball in stride and bounced back. He had shaken even Rodney with that move, and he had executed just like always only ten years later. He was as surprised as everyone else. A crowd was starting to form.

The ball bounced on the dusty midway. Tiny clouds puffed into existence each time. Johnny stood behind the can again. This time he didn't even stop to square his shoulders. He raised the ball overhead, left his feet and tossed the ball high as if over a defender. The ball soared up and into the hoop again. The net snapped with a single whispering *fwhip*. The gathered crowd of people clapped for him as if he had made a long putt on a golf course. It was back. That rush of competition filled him. He jogged up to the barrier and waited for the ball to roll down to Larry at the bottom of the game.

"Not too bad," Larry told him, genuinely impressed. "You sure you don't wanna call it a day. You got a crowd watchin' you now."

"Then we should give them a show," Johnny said. He caught Larry's pass with his fingertips and set it back down to a dribble. He brought the first bounce up and whipped the ball around his back. The ball hit the ground again. Slowly he envisioned the old black cleats he wore to practice in his yard. The ground was hard, but the surface was dirt and still slid under his Converse sneakers, so the cleats allowed him to cut and juke without falling.

In his driveway, Johnny could be something he couldn't anywhere else: the best. The smell of humidity and the sound of cicadas and frogs filled the night air, a symphony of completely pure Southern life. Rodney Malone ruled the Nowheresville hallway top to bottom, and Johnny's dad took over at home. But late at night in the dirt patch in his front yard, Johnny was the greatest basketball player in the world. He would sneak out there late at night when everyone else was asleep—three, four in the morning—and he'd practice until the sun came up. He always pretended he was asleep when Merle woke him. Many times Johnny'd barely make it back to bed before Merle got up. He'd still be sweaty, and Merle would think he was sick.

"You pussin' out, boy?" He'd ask Johnny.

"No, sir," Johnny'd say. "Just got hot is all."

That'd be that.

Johnny didn't have a hoop at his house. The only kid in the neighborhood who did was Eli Barns, who was too close to Rodney for Johnny's comfort. So Johnny painted a large black dot roughly ten feet up the trunk of a pine tree near the dirt patch. The dot didn't face the house so Merle never really noticed it, and when he did he just assumed it was a knot or a dead spot in the trunk.

Johnny would dribble from one end of the dirt patch to the tree shaking off imaginary defenders. He saw them reaching for the ball, his ball. He had done this for as long as he can remember. Even when his mom was around he was bouncing a ball.

The dot on the tree didn't make the best hoop, so much like his handling, a lot of the practice relied heavily on Johnny's imagination. He couldn't actually see the defenders, but Johnny wasn't especially tall so he imagined having to leap higher than them. The arc on the ball was much higher than anyone else he knew. The ball seemed to hang in the air as if taunting the defenders it soared over. Its descent was slow and sped up as it reached the black dot on the tree. Instead of hitting it and ricocheting back to him, the ball would graze the dot, much like it did the rim during a game as it fell through the net. The trick was to leave his hand up where the ball was released, for luck. Johnny did this for hours, nearly every night, even when it rained. In fact, he preferred those rainy nights, because those were the nights he didn't have to sweep the divots from his cleats out of the surface of the dirt.

There were nights when Johnny simply couldn't separate reality from the imaginary players in his head, and as long as they were there, Johnny scored on them. That dirt patch in front of his house was Johnny's favorite place in the world outside the gym. He crossed the dirt patch, shaking defenders. The lane was closed, no way through or around to the goal. Three seconds on the clock and Nowheresville High was down by two. He was behind the three-point line. Now or never. Johnny faked in and pulled the ball back. The defender stumbled back. Johnny left his feet and released the ball.

The arc of the ball was so high that the night sky above his dirt patch in the woods brightened to a late afternoon orange above Dandy D's Carnival Funland. The smell of corndogs came rushing back to him. Out of the corner of his eye, Harriet's hands covered her mouth in a picture-perfect visual of excitement. There were other people there also. He had developed a crowd of about twenty-five people. Johnny looked around at them, his hand still in the air.

The ball came down. The net popped that note of complete satisfaction. The crowd cheered. It was more than the typical golf clap. It was a loud cheer. The sound was as though he had just won the state championship again. Harriet walked toward him cheering.

Johnny lowered his hand and put his arm around her. "I believe you ordered a prize?"

"I did," she said. She could not be more proud of him.

Everyone deserves a few really great moments. Hell, even Larry was impressed and clapping on his way up the ladder to retrieve the big, black bear hanging over the goal. This was a particularly great moment in Johnny's life. It was the start of his life here. And if it could start this well—with a win—it might even last that way forever. First impressions have a lot of power, you know.

Johnny stood in the surrounding crowd, his wife in his arms, people cheering for him for doing something he truly loved. He swelled with pride. He almost didn't care if he received the prize. Of course he did though, because it wasn't for him. It was for the woman he loved.

I hope you keep that in mind. There is a great deal more to his story than this. This is the last good moment before he came to me. I think it's important that I was part of it. See, he does belong with us. Hell, he's more involved than even me at this point.

He belongs here.

The crowd continued as Johnny and Harriet made their way to Larry at the barrier. He was holding the bear. They still have him. Johnny bowed his head, and in an act of showmanship, Larry bestowed the stuffed bear unto Harriet. She took and hugged it tightly for the first time of millions.

"I love it!" Harriet said. She gave the stuffed black bear a tight hug. "I'm naming him Griz. Griz the grizzly bear."

Johnny warmed. "It's perfect. What should we do now?"

"I think it's time for some rides," Harriet smiled.

They walked toward the carousel. Harriet bounced with joy. She held Johnny's hand in one hand, and Griz in the other.

3

Carousel

The carousel is the first ride you come to from the main entrance of the Funland. It's there because you expect it to be. It sets an expectation that not many things in the Funland can do. You see, the only people who ride the carousel are the people who genuinely wanna ride it.

The children, easy. They see those horses, and they go silly. The special thing about Dandy D's is that we don't just stop at horses. We got lions, tigers, and bears, just like that movie. We got wolves and deer, even ostriches. Could you imagine reading those National Geographic magazines or going to the zoo where they keep big ferocious kitty cats, and then coming to the Funland and *ridin'* one of those beasts? Taming it like a pup. Ridin' it around like a bicycle. And we got'm all. If we don't got'm, we get'm. Everybody finds an animal they wanna ride.

More than anything else, the kids help set the tone for the

entire visit. Sure, the adults ride, but they are a very slim minority. They don't care what animal they ride. Most of them are only there to make sure their toddlers don't fall off, or get scared when the ride starts spinning. The kids are key. The kids are the ones who wear everything on their sleeves. All it takes are some bright colors and animals to get the smiles on their faces and laughter in the air. Set it all in motion and passersby get living slideshow of dozens of happy children.

Even those adults who don't care what animal they ride are riding because they feel the same way Johnny and Harriet felt. Just like kids. They don't care what they look like to other people. They're just there to have fun with each other. Being lovers. One smile breeds more smiles. That's your key to success in our business. Find something simple. Something everyone loves, to set the mood. Everyone on the carousel loves being on the carousel.

Johnny and Harriet waited in line, holding hands the entire time. Griz played the part of their adopted child. All around them real children were bouncing with excitement. Kids shouted at their friends as they sped by on their wild animals. The air filled with innocent calls of who was going to ride which animal next.

"I'm gonna ride the horse!"

"I call the tiger!"

"I'm getting the cheetah!"

He never would have admitted it, but Johnny secretly hoped he and Harriet would get through the line in time to snag a ride on the wolf.

The wolf was always his favorite animal.

There was a documentary film at the park where someone had filmed live wolves in the snow somewhere in Alaska. The narrator, played by Principal Gordon, read random facts about the *canis lupus tundrarum*. Johnny sat with Jerry close enough to the projector that he could hear the narrator as a separate voice from the speaker. He fell into a trance listening to the voice and watching the projection. He never forgot the way they came out of the woods in packs, the way there were always more eyes in the darkness than Johnny expected. There was always one more pair. They were always watching from the darkness.

He remembered going to see that movie with someone. Jerry was a neighborhood kid. He was smaller than Johnny. He couldn't remember very many times they got together, but he remembered the kid's face very well. Jerry was a little older, and there was the beginnings of a mustache on his face. It looked kind of like one of those milk mustaches. They had ridden to the park on their bikes. The principal of the high school had built a screen out of ladders, brooms, and a bed sheet. The movie itself was silent, but there was a script read into a microphone. The video lasted for thirty-five minutes. The narrator hadn't paced the facts correctly so the final five minutes were silent. That's when everything else in the world disappeared.

The wolves sprinted through the snow after some small animal that was cut off at the bottom where the sheet didn't reach the ground. Johnny roamed the woods of Alaska with the wolfpack by his side. He was one of them. They darted through the snowy forest with blinding speed. Johnny had never seen anything so ferociously artistic in his life. Those few silent minutes in the park changed everything about how he saw the food chain. Johnny stared at the screen with his mouth agape for longer than he thought. The sheet went dark before he realized he hadn't moved for so long that his feet had fallen asleep.

"Ha!" Rodney said. "Little bitch looks like he's waiting to put something in his mouth."

Eli and Brett barked laughter like hyenas. They fell over each other as they sauntered toward Johnny and Jerry in the center of the park.

Johnny shrank back into himself a little.

Eli and Brett started pushing each other.

"Get off me, queer," Brett said.

"I'm not queer. You're queer," Eli said, tackling Brett. Johnny could tell now that the three of them—Eli and Brett at the very least—were stoned out of their minds.

"Hey," Rodney said, falling over them. "You're both a bunch of queers. Get off me. Leave me out of your bedroom bullshit."

"Rodney Malone!"

"What?" Rodney shouted in great defiance at the angry voice.

Johnny turned to see who had shouted Rodney's name. It was Principal Gordon. His mustache twitched with the anger allotted by the pitiful amount of power accompanying the principal's desk at a small town school. The wind tousled his thin hair. "You watch your mouth, Rodney, or I'll have a talk with Coach Whitford. Do you hear me?"

"What are y'all gonna talk about, Quincy, huh?" Rodney let out a stupid, pot-laced giggle.

Principal Gordon's mouth dropped open. "Have you been smoking goof-butts, son?"

"Goof what?" Eli mocked.

"Are you *high*?" Principal Gordon elaborated.

"Oh, shit," Brett said.

"Run!" Rodney shouted, still unable to stop from giggling.

The three of them fumbled to their feet and hobbled out of the park into the eerie nothingness beyond the lights.

"You boys need to go too," Principal Gordon told Johnny and Jerry.

"Yes, sir," Johnny said. He was unable to stop smiling. Out of fear that Principal Gordon would accuse him of smoking "goof-butts," Johnny rushed onto his bicycle and sped off into the night without looking back.

On the way back to their neighborhood, Johnny energetically praised the movie. He spoke so quickly his words jumbled together as they rushed from his mouth into the open air of the dirt road. Jerry wasn't as excited, but he tried his hardest to keep pace.

"That was so cool!" Johnny shouted.

"Could you imagine being a wolf?" Jerry said. "What do you think it's like?"

Wild was the first word that came to Johnny's head. That didn't seem like the appropriate word. That was something for which his dad would call him a pussy. "I think it would be awesome! I would be leader of the pack."

"If I could be a wolf, I'd be fast as lightning," Jerry said. He lowered his head and pedaled faster through the dark.

"Not as fast as me!" Johnny shouted. He stood on the pedals, rocking the bike side to side beneath him to reach maximum speed. He passed Jerry in a flash. Leaves rustled under their wheels. Johnny began to pull away from Jerry.

"Remember the howl?" Jerry called.

Johnny did.

The principal had played a recording of real, actual wolves before the narration, and replayed the recording during the part about wolf packs. It started with a single howl.

AAAWWWRRRROOOOOO!

Then another voice joined the first. And another. Soon there were six, maybe even seven wolves howling away.

AAAWWWRRRROOOOOO!

Johnny had never been so entertained. He wanted a copy of the reel and the projector. The thought of stealing it crossed his mind for a moment before he was able to push it back away. He was a fan, not a criminal.

"Oh, yeah," Johnny answered. His excitement was boiling. "*AAAWWRRRROOOOO! OW OW OOOOOOWWWW!*"

"*AAWWRROOO!*" Jerry joined him.

They were like a wolf pack of their own.

Johnny sat back on his bike seat. He breathed deeply and released a howl that a real pack could hear from miles away and start howling with him.

As the call of his animal instinct tapered off into the night, the woods answered him. The sound of cicadas tore through the air like an alarm.

SKREEEEEEEEEE!

"Geez, it's like we pissed them off or something," Johnny nearly shouted over the terrible sound. His hand instinctively went to one ear to block the racket.

"It's just bugs," Jerry said as he pedaled faster to catch up. "They're like roaches. I don't remember what they call them, but they're harmless."

Out of the corner of his eye, Johnny saw a flicker—eyes—in the darkness behind the trees. Watching him. Whatever those eyes belonged to, it was watching them. The fun in Johnny's voice took a hit and faltered slightly. "Whoa," he said. "Did you see that?"

"What?" Jerry asked. His tone was upbeat, hinting that he didn't see the eyes. He didn't know they were being watched. "What was it?"

"I don't know," Johnny said with growing concern.

"Do you think it was a wolf?" Jerry's tone remained lighthearted.

Johnny didn't think it was a wolf. Wolves were scary but not like this.

Ahead of them, something darted across the dirt road and into the woods. It was quick and blended into the night. Johnny almost didn't see it. Something hard filled his stomach then. Fear.

"That! Did you see it?"

"No, I didn't see anything. *AAWWRROOO*—," Jerry was cut off then. His bike's chain snapped. One end tangled into the gear of his back wheel. The other end whipped up and raked across the back of his calf muscle. Jerry shrieked in pain. He fell back on the seat so hard the he lost balance, and his bike toppled over onto the ground. Jerry hit the ground with a dusty *thunk.*

Johnny spun around so quickly that he almost fell off his own bike. "What happened? Are you okay?"

Jerry groaned in pain. "I think my chain locked up on me. Something got my leg."

Johnny dismounted and propped his bike back on the kickstand. His eyes darted wildly to both sides of the road. The sound of the cicadas rose and fell. Breathed and died off. The sound was like something living all its own. Hundreds of buzzing insects brayed their unison alarm through the woods. Only the occasional off-key voice stuck out to him as he made his way to Jerry. The closer he got to Jerry, the more Johnny was able to pick out a pattern. At first he only heard one long, uninterrupted cry.

rrrEEEEEEEEEEEEEEE!

As he moved, more and more of the bugs were joining in on the rhythm. It was still one long voice, but in the middle there were three quick breaks.

rrrEEEEEEEE EEE EEE EEEEEEEEEE!

Johnny recognized it as a howl of their own. With every step closer to Jerry, the pattern became more pronounced.

But these were bugs. Jerry said it himself, bugs. Harmless, like roaches. Johnny knew bugs didn't know how to howl, but it sounded almost like they were mocking him.

No, Johnny thought. *They're bugs. Harmless.*

A fallen branch snapped beside him. Johnny jerked toward the sound. He didn't see anything. He couldn't hear anything else over the drone of the bugs.

"Ah, man," Jerry said. "I'm bleeding. My parents are going to kill me. They said they weren't going to buy me any more pants if I kept playing rough in these."

"Are you hurt?"

"Yeah, it hurts."

"Can you get up? This place is starting to freak me out."

Jerry laughed. "You scared?"

"Shut up," Johnny said, playing cool. "I saw something."

"I didn't see anything. I think the film got into your head."

Leaves rustled behind Johnny. Something was running through the woods. He could barely hear it over the droning. He could tell whatever it was had run down the road away from them. He was able to relax a little then. The sound of rustling leaves stopped.

"Johnny," Jerry said from the ground. He pointed behind Johnny in the direction of where the sound was leading. "There it is."

Johnny whipped around and saw it. It was long and emaciated. Tufts of what he assumed was fur dangled from beneath it, dragging on the ground. Its figure was less than solid. It was more like smoke. It went in and out keeping the thing's shape more of a general outline. The only thing that remained consistent was the thing's eyes. They reflected a bright green light. It looked different though. The reflection wasn't just a solid circle like every other animal's he had seen in the dark. There was a pupil. They weren't reflections; they were actual irises. He was looking at that thing's eyes. Even if it blinked, the green circles would momentarily vanish then reappear right where they were before. More than anything else, that made Johnny nervous. It meant the thing was watching them. Johnny didn't want to believe that. He didn't want to believe that he was seeing eyes that didn't reflect but glowed in the dark.

Johnny blinked away from the sight and refocused. The thing in the road looked more solid now. The eyes were the same though.

"It's watching us," Johnny mumbled to himself.

"What do we do, Johnny?"

"Can you get up?" Johnny watched every move the thing in the road made even though it remained still. Johnny thought that maybe it really was a statue, but then it moved again.

Jerry struggled to his feet. He dusted off his pants and winced at the pain in his calf. "I'm good. I don't know if my bike is going to make it though."

The thing reared up on his hind legs and walked a few clumsy steps toward them, hobbling like a gigantic bear. It wasn't thick enough to be a bear though. It was more like the skeleton of a bear wearing its own skin. It dropped back down on its front legs coughing. Johnny saw something like phlegm flying out of its mouth.

"I think it's sick," Johnny said.

"What *is* that thing?"

"I can't tell."

"It's not a wolf. It's too big. It's like a bear or something."

"It's looks like a panther. But it's too big to be a panther."

"What do you want to do?"

"I think we can scare it away. It's sick. It's doesn't want to fight."

"Scare it away?" Jerry said sarcastically. "Like, we're gonna wear a bed sheet and pretend to be a ghost?"

"No," Johnny said. "We can scream at it like the hunters did the wolves in the film. We can probably just run it off."

"What do we say?"

"I have no idea."

"*Hey you!*" Jerry shouted. It was easy to hear now that the cicadas had, for the most part, stopped droning. Jerry's voice echoes through the woods. "*Get out of here, all right?*"

The thing in the road surprised them then. As the coughs tapered off, a new type of wheezing sound replaced it. It still hacked, but the sound was unmistakable. It was laughing at them. But that couldn't be. First the bugs, now this thing? Mocking them. Johnny thought they must have gotten high while standing too close to Rodney. He was hearing things. Yes, hearing and seeing things.

Johnny shook it off and banished the fear from his voice. "*Get out of here!*"

The thing stopped hacking then. It braced itself as if for an attack.

"*Yeah, get!*" Jerry added.

"I think we freaked it out," Johnny said. "We're going to

have to run toward it."

"Why would we do that?"

"Because if we just stay here it's not going to move. My bike is over there, if that thing tears it up, my dad will beat me."

"I can't run," Jerry said with a tremor in his voice.

"That's fine. I'll go first. You just have to look like you're running with me so it thinks we're both coming for it."

"Aw, man," Jerry groaned.

"It's best not to think about it. You can do it. I'm going to count to three."

"Aw man," Jerry repeated.

"One…"

rrrrEEEEEEEEEEEEEEE!

The cicadas roared to life again in that same orchestral bray. Johnny would never think of that sound the same way. He could hear the individual bugs mocking him with their own version of the wolf pack howl.

rrrrEEEEEEEEEE EEE EEE EEEEEEEEE!

Jerry shouted a startled yelp.

"Just ignore the bugs. They're just roaches, remember?"

"Yeah," Jerry said. The bugs were at the back of his mind in that moment.

"One…two…three!"

The two of them bolted as quick as they could down the dirt road, screaming incoherent nonsense as they stormed toward the thing in the road.

"*Aahhhh! You better move!*" Johnny shrieked at the top of his nearly empty lungs. He had never felt such a powerful combination of fear, adrenaline, and lunacy all at once. He felt vines and limbs reaching for his legs on the side of the road. One tangled around his ankle, but he ripped free of it without breaking stride. "*I'm coming for you!*"

The thing that wasn't a bear or a panther or a wolf stepped back and reinforced its hold on the ground. It wasn't trying to attack them though. Its body language was that of a playful dog. It didn't have a tail, but Johnny could easily imagine one wagging behind it.

Johnny gained ground on the thing, screaming louder. Just as the thing's features began to take form, it darted back into the woods. The cicadas' drone died down low enough for Johnny to hear that wheezing, hacking laugh again. It was an old laugh, and behind it there was the very distinct sound of a baby's giggle.

"What the hell is going on?" Johnny asked no one in particular.

"It left!" Jerry said through heaving breaths. He was limping toward Johnny, holding his bike beside him. "You were right. We scared it off."

"It's probably best we hurry up and get out of here anyway." Johnny kicked up his bike's stand and began quickly walking to the clearing where his house waited in the dark. He had reached it when Jerry spoke up behind him.

"I can't make it, man," Jerry said. He collapsed onto the ground, which was the very last thing Johnny wanted him to do.

"You have to get up. Come on." Johnny lowered the kickstand and left his bike to help his friend. Johnny hurried over and pulled Jerry to his feet. His voice was stern enough to hide the trembling fear beneath it. "Here put your arm around me."

Jerry held himself up between his bike and Johnny. Between the two of them, Jerry was able to keep his weight off his injured leg completely.

The cicadas fell silent. The only sounds were the wind in the trees and the croaking toads. Johnny couldn't figure out what had just happened.

"What was that thing," Johnny breathed.

"What thing?" Jerry answered, dumb confusion painted across his face.

"What do you mean? That..." Johnny stalled. He reached for the thought, but nothing came to him. He couldn't even remember what the thing looked like. It was as though in the panic of getting out of the woods the idea just fell out of his pocket and lay on the dirty ground. That was perfectly fine with Johnny. The only thing that stuck was that they were freaking out. It probably wasn't something Johnny wanted to remember anyway.

Jerry's house was only a few hundred feet further down the dirt road than Johnny's. Johnny thought he could help Jerry and make it home without his dad waking up, but then the porch light illuminated. Johnny had never gotten used to seeing it, and he jumped. The screen door hit the side of the house with a sharp *fwap*, announcing the arrival of Merle Davis. Johnny hated how the dirty yellow light bulb always made it seem like he was trying to hide what he was doing.

"What's going on out there, boy?" Merle called.

"I'm helping Jerry get home."

"He got two feet, don't he?" Merle let the question sit in the open air. "Why don't you let him walk?"

In the silence of the night, Johnny left Jerry's side and watched as his friend hobbled up the road. He stood in the dirt patch in front of his house waiting for his dad to give another command.

"Where's your bike, boy?"

"It's right over there."

"Why is it over there?"

"I was helping Jerry get home. He got—"

"Why don't you get your bike, and get your ass in bed?"

Johnny ran for his bike. The buzzing grew the closer he got to it. He kicked up the stand, but something caught his eye before he could mount the seat. He shook it away and rode the bike to the house and parked it in the back where he always did. The back door was locked, so he walked around to the front of the house. Merle waited for him in the doorway.

Merle cleared his throat, and took the last swig of his beer. "I don't want you around that queer no more."

"He's my—"

"I didn't ask you what he was. I told you I didn't want him around here."

"Yes, sir."

Merle tossed the beer can in the yard and spit before turning back into the house. "Damn queers!" He shouted and slammed the door to his bedroom behind him.

Johnny waited a moment before entering the house. The

springs on his dad's bed strained as they took on his weight. Johnny quietly walked to his room, but sleep didn't come for a while. He couldn't take his mind off the film he saw. The way they hunted. The way they weaved through the trees. The way they acted like a team. He dropped onto his twin bed. His body was tired, but his heart drummed.

I wish we were the wolves instead of the tigers, Johnny thought. His heart rate slowed.

"Which one do you want to ride?" a voice came to him. His mother's? No.

Johnny slipped slowly to sleep.

Johnny was the leader of the pack. He found their prey. Three small white fluffs in the snow. He slowly moved forward, not making a sound.

"Johnny, sweetie?" Harriet said.

Johnny pounced. They had captured their prey. They ate like animals. His instinct kicked in, and the pack leader howled.

AAAWWRRRROOOOOO OW OW OOOOOOWWWWW!

"Johnny," Harriet said, shaking him back to the present. She held Griz like a baby on her hip.

"I'm sorry, what'd I miss?" They were standing at the front of the line. His hand rested on the railing that kept people from walking out onto the revolving platform.

"You were singing," Harriet said, giggling.

"I was?" Johnny blushed.

"Yeah," Harriet said. "Just some oo's but it was singing."

"Sorry, I guess I just zoned out." Johnny couldn't help

but laugh at himself.

"It's fine," Harriet said. "So which animal do you want to ride?"

"I think I'll ride the wolf."

"Oo, scary," Harriet said. She playfully growled at Johnny and pounced on him.

He kissed her forehead and hugged her close to him. "Which one do you want to ride?"

"Well, preferably whatever is closest to the wolf. Let's see…" Harriet feigned genuine pensive thought. "Oh look at that! It's a tiger." She growled at Johnny once again.

"You like tigers?"

"Well, it is the closest to the wolf," Harriet said. "But I've loved tigers since you and me were tigers ourselves. Do you remember those days?"

The smell of bubblegum and peppermint tickled Johnny's nose again. He was taken back to Phil's Drive-thru. His face was sweaty from the grill, and his hands had pruned from washing the ice cream machine parts. Outside on the tables Harriet sat eating her salted chicken strips and her unsalted French fries. The other cheerleaders were huddled with her on one end of the picnic table, and the football players were at the other. Their showboating and childish games were almost ritualistic. They had a leader, his name was Lloyd Barns, cousin of Rodney Malone's lackey, Eli. He told stories with one foot on the table and hunched over to bring everyone's attention to him and him alone. Johnny heard him through the glass.

"…I mean this guy was two-twenty a least," Lloyd said,

straightening his letterman jacket. A single swipe set him back to perfectly cool.

"At least!" a cheerleader added.

"That's right, so he's coming at me. So I put my hand out to push him away, and he just bowls in on me. He has me by the arm, and I'm trying like everything to shake him off of me."

There was a gasp from the cheerleaders. All but Harriet.

"So, finally I pull my arm free, right?" Lloyd continued. "And Johnson is coming across the field and he's wide open. So I let it fly." Lloyd threw an imaginary ball over his audience's head. And he waited. *Always wait for them to ask.* He told himself.

"So what happened?" a cheerleader asked.

"Well, of course, Johnson caught it," one of the other football players said. "We won the game!"

A cheer went out from the table, and Johnny was secretly jealous of them. The only time he had seen the court at the time was when the two teams came together to shake hands at the end of the game. But like I said before, Nowheresville High used the same cheerleaders for the basketball games as for the football games. So Johnny got to see his true love cheering for him, even if it wasn't for him specifically. They were team wins after all.

Johnny didn't know Harriet was even a cheerleader until the first time he laced up his tennis shoes sporting the blue and gold tigers uniform. She had missed the first game for some reason, but at the second, she came in with the rest of the squad.

This was his freshman season, and he didn't know a soul on the squad, on the team, or in the stands. So he watched Harriet.

Her uniform was clean royal blue, and the skirt had a white hem at the bottom. Across the breast there were the three letters indicating that Nowheresville High was whom she was there to cheer on to victory. Her ponytail bounced behind her head the exact same way the rest of their ponytails did. Johnny didn't see it that way though. She wasn't just another one of them.

In fact, that was the first time he imagined winning the game with a last second three-pointer. The crowd would rush the floor and lift him up over their heads. He would ask to be put down next to her, and they would share a kiss at center court.

That was the second game of the year though. There would never be that kind of reaction for the second game of the season even if it did end with a last second three-point buzzer beater. That didn't slow him from thinking about her hands in his though, or his arm around her in a sweet sophomoric embrace as they left the gym.

The buzzer resounded throughout the gym, snapping Johnny back to the game that was now coming back from halftime. He was actually standing on the court. A freshman standing on the court? There must be some kind of mistake.

He was on defense, and across the court the star center tipped a shot and picked the ball out of the air for a turnover. Johnny bolted to the opposite end of the court. The offense set up in formation, and the guard called the play.

Johnny was actually going to get the ball. He was to wait for the pick, curl around and expect the ball to come in the paint for an easy layup. Johnny was only a freshman, and he was actually getting the ball.

He felt the pick and spun immediately around his man. He focused on the guard who was a little late on the pass, but Johnny was able to correct for the error. Johnny caught the ball and left his feet. A defender leapt at the same time, knocking Johnny off balance. The ball left his hand and bounced off the rim.

Johnny was able to catch himself before falling to the ground. The referee's whistle pierced the air and continued to ring long after the sound had stopped.

"Defensive foul, number thirteen," the referee called.

Number thirteen raised his arms in a "What gives?" gesture, but Johnny only clapped and took his position at the foul line. A quiet golf clap spread around the bleachers as the referee passed Johnny the ball.

Johnny bounced it once. That's all he needed really, and even that was for show. With his feet and shoulders square, Johnny raised the ball over his head and let it fly. The ball sank into the rim, flicking the net.

One for one.

Another bored cheer spread through the gym. No one ever cares about free throws.

The referee passed Johnny the ball again. Johnny bounced the ball once, for show, and sank the second shot.

Two for two.

Johnny was a shooter. Of course, he made them both.

The other team drove the ball down the court. They ran a very similar play and Johnny sniffed it out. When the guard passed on the inside, Johnny leaped into the paint and broke the pass up. The ball nearly went out of bounds, but a player on the opposite team scooped it up. He passed inside, and the player drew a foul on the way to a layup, only this player made the fouled shot. Johnny clapped for the sake of showmanship and took his place around the foul line.

The buzzer blared, and Johnny was substituted out for the starter.

He took his place on the bench and stayed there until the end of the game. His stat sheet read:

Shots M: 0, Shots A: 0 FTA: 2, FTM: 2, pts. 2, assist: 0, fouls: 0, steals: 0, blocks : 0

Johnny had never been more proud of a two-point performance in his life, and it would be the last time he would be so proud. He saw a girl and scored two points. So even if she didn't see the rest of his game, the chances of her seeing one of those two shots were pretty good. He kept an eye out for her after the final buzzer, but the cheerleaders had gone home in the third quarter when the tigers started to run away with the lead. That's okay though. The season was long. Johnny knew he'd get his chance.

Besides, it all worked out in the end. Here he stood with his beautiful lady on his arm, waiting to ride the carousel of all things. He couldn't remember exactly when, but sometime amidst all those games, Harriet did meet him at half court for that kiss. Gosh it was so long ago that Johnny couldn't even remember their first kiss? That couldn't be right. He remembered all of them. Surely, he could remember that one.

The children laughing on the carousel groaned together as the platform came to a complete stop. There were cries for one more ride, and parents telling children that there were other rides to go on, all ending in cheerful exits. Dandy D's: You'll never go home unhappy.

"You two ready?" the carny asked. He looked familiar to Johnny. He would've sworn that he literally just saw this face behind the barrier of the basketball hoop game. This man looked exactly like Larry. Only this time, his suit was green instead of blue.

"Oh, we're ready!"

"First in line, you picked out your animal?" The man's excitement was contagious.

"We did," Johnny said.

"Where ya headed?" The carney looked at them with a caricature expression of inquisition.

"I'm going to the tiger, and he's going to the wolf." Harriet giggled again. Harriet held Griz up to the carney. "By the way, do you have a place I can leave my bear?"

"Sure thing," the carney said. He stepped to the side, presenting a wooden crate that had the words "Prize Waiting Area" written across it in blue marker.

"Why, thank you," Harriet said, gently laying Griz in the bin.

"You two have fun," the carney instructed. Somehow,

right in front of Harriet and Johnny there was a wolf and tiger waiting for them. Then the carny addressed the rest of the line. "Here we go, folks! It's time to *RIIIIDE!* But be wary. They's wild animals afoot."

A cheer greeted this from the children in line.

"Fly!" the carney shouted.

"Come on!" Harriet grabbed Johnny's hand.

The metal gate swung open, and a stampede of children followed after Johnny and Harriet. They mounted their animals while still holding one another's hand.

"This is going to be so much fun!" Harriet said.

"I know!" Johnny said, matching her excitement. She looked even more beautiful than ever in the glow of the yellow lights above her.

"Don't forget your buckle, cowboy," Harriet said, pointing to one half of the harness dangling from Johnny's wolf.

"You think we'll actually need these?"

"I don't want you to fall off," she grinned.

The ride started up. The platform began its rotation. The children on the ride shrieked their elation, and Harriet joined them. She couldn't help but to laugh like they did, and Johnny joined them.

The wind blew Johnny's black hair away from his forehead. The revolution sped up. Johnny tightened his hold on the pole. He glanced over at Harriet who was snarling like a tiger in his direction. She swiped a playful claw at him. Johnny's animal instinct kicked in again.

"*AAAWWWRRRROOOOO! OW! OW! OOOOWWWW!*"

Harriet burst into shocked laughter.

All the children around them began acting like whichever animal they were riding. Jaguars roared, horses brayed, there was even a trumpeting elephant on the other side of the platform.

"Look what you started," Harriet said.

"No, ma'am," Johnny answered. "That was all you."

Harriet reached for him. She pulled Johnny closer to her and kissed his lips.

"I love you," she said.

"I love you, too," he answered.

"Yah!" Harriet shouted, and spurred her tiger.

The calliope music wound quicker and matched the speed of the revolving platform. Johnny thought that strange pipe organ-style music was eerie. It didn't fit the tone of merriment. He thought it belonged accompanying a street performer or creepy uncle's visit. It definitely didn't welcome a comfortable feeling.

Johnny leaned back, trying to tune out the noise. The wind blew all around him. It was a familiar feeling. The breeze always seemed to blow the coldest when Johnny walked home from basketball practice when he was soaked in sweat. But this wasn't the same kind of breeze.

A rush of warm air touched Johnny's face. It grew to an unusual heat for this time of day. The warmth on his face moved to the back of his neck. The breeze changed directions. Johnny opened his eyes and was greeted by a bright yellow sun. It peaked up just above their house. Behind him, his mother pushed him on the rope swing connected to the branch above his head. They were laughing.

"Do you want to go higher?" Edie asked.

"Yeah, momma," little Johnny said. The words were jumbled in his head. He was only three so sentences were new to him. "I wanna fly to the sun."

"Silly, boy," Edie said. "That would burn your fingers."

"But I'm a big boy. I'm strong."

"The sun is too hot for you though, sweetheart."

"But I'm a big boy," little Johnny reiterated.

"Well, okay then," Edie said. "Here goes nothing!" Edie forced an *oof* to make sure little Johnny knew that more effort was being made. In reality though, if he had gone any higher, it was only an inch or two.

"I'm going to the sun!" Johnny shouted.

"Fly, sweetheart, fly," Edie giggled with her son.

And then a thought came to Johnny. *Does it really hurt when you touch it?* There was really only one way to know. Johnny reached his little finger toward the blinding yellow ball. Nothing happened.

"What are you pointing at, sweetheart?"

Johnny stretched his arm into the sky. He didn't feel anything but the warm rays on his face. He put his arm around the rope and reached further.

"Honey, no, don't do that," Edie said trying to stop him.

When Johnny reached the height of his arc, the seat of the swing went back without him. When he started back down toward the Earth, he was laying at a forty-five degree angle.

In the way of mothers, Edie launched herself toward her baby boy, stretching her arms before her. She was able to get a hold of little Johnny's waistband before the swing tripped her, sending both of them to the ground. Johnny fell onto the sand beneath the swings while his mother landed on her hands and knees, taking the brunt of the fall without the extra arm to help stop her momentum.

Johnny wanted to start crying, but something stopped him. It was the look on his mother's face. The pain in her grimacing face pierced right through to his heart. He instinctively wanted to comfort her, but he didn't know how. Three-year-olds don't know how to do a lot of things their instincts tell them to do. "Momma? Did you get hurt?"

Edie breathed heavily. A tear squeezed between her clinched eyelids. She opened her bloodshot eyes. The tone in her voice was soaked in anger, but she concentrated on hiding it.

You will not be like his father.

"I'm fine, sweetheart. But you can't do that anymore. Ever again. Do you hear me?"

"I'm sorry, Momma." Johnny rolled over to his hands and knees. He crawled up to his mother the way a dog would. He put his arm around her, and shed a sympathetic tear for her.

"It's okay, sweetheart," Edie assured him. Luckily, her baby boy was quick to learn from a mistake. "Don't cry. You're a big boy. Just promise me you'll never do that again."

"I promise."

"Good," she told him. "You want to help Momma back to her feet?"

Johnny reached out his hand, and Edie took it. She stood using her son's hand for nothing more than a lesson in being a gentleman. Edie dusted off her hands and skirt.

"Now, come on," Edie said. She took Johnny's hand and led him across the dirt patch back into the house. "We got all dirty, and your daddy's about to be home. Let's get washed up and ready for supper."

"Mmm, supper!" Johnny hollered. "What's supper tonight?"

"We're having spaghetti!"

"Psketty has worms," Johnny groaned.

"Psketty doesn't have worms," Edie said, pulling Johnny to her and tickling his belly.

"Yes huh," he said through heaving laughing breaths.

"You got worms in *you*," Edie tackled him to the ground with her tickling fingers.

A rumbling engine slowly crescendoed from down the road. The trees blocked the sight of the pale green Ford, but Edie and Johnny both knew that the sound meant Daddy was home.

"Up! Up, up, up," Edie told Johnny. She rushed him to his feet. She dusted off his clothes and straightened his hair as best she could before the chrome bumper shined around the corner. Then the full car came into view. The horn blared two quick hits.

womp wooomp

"Daddy!" little Johnny shouted.

"That's right," Edie said. "That's daddy."

The Ford rambled into the driveway and Merle cut the

engine. The door swung open, and Merle stepped out of the car. He held a bouquet of flowers for his wife. The breeze crinkled the paper wrapped around it. "How's my family doing?"

"Daddy!" Johnny ran to him and hugged his waist.

"We had a great day," Edie told him. She joined the rest of her family by the car. Merle handed her the flowers, and she made a show of smelling them and saying how beautiful they were. She thought maybe they were plastic, but at least he tried. It was good to see that spirits were high after a long week in Baton Rouge. She was surprised. He rarely came home this happy, even when he worked at the plant in town. She hugged him and felt something in the back of his waistband. "What is that?"

"I got a gun," Merle answered like a kid with a new toy.

"What for?" Edie felt the handle, confirming that it was a gun.

"I think if they got me making the tanks, I ought to be allowed a weapon. It's patriotic."

"Okay, then," she said. And there was nothing else to say. Merle wasn't the kind of man to change his mind on a decision he had made. "How was work?"

"They took me off the ball bearings this week. Now I'm on the axels."

"Is that right?" Edie said. She didn't know what either of those were, but if it was the cause for Merle's happiness, she didn't want to look too far into it.

"Yes," Merle said. Then he shifted his attention to his son. "I ain't gonna have to fumble around with those small parts anymore. My hands won't hurt so much, ain't that right?"

"Right!" Johnny added.

"So what's for dinner?"

"I was going to make spaghetti," Edie said.

"Sounds good," Merle said.

"So what was it like working on the military tanks and boats?" Edie asked, sweetly.

"I tell you one thing," Merle said. "Got my manhood going. Testosterone or whatever. Why don't we, uh, take a nap before you get to dinner." He patted her backside.

"Oh, my," Edie pretended to swoon.

"Then you can wake me up when supper's ready."

"We can do that."

"Psketty!" Little Johnny said.

Edie let her guard down in a rare moment of family bliss. She kissed Merle and massaged his shoulder.

"Why don't you go swing for a minute, buddy? Me and your mom need to be alone a minute."

"I can swing myself?"

"Yes," Edie said. Her tone was now authoritative. "You promise to be careful?"

"I will."

"Have fun, sweetheart," Edie said. Deep down she knew this would more than likely end with Johnny running into the house with a scraped elbow. It'd only be a minute though. Maybe not even that long. She'd be right back.

Johnny awkwardly ran across the yard, tripping only once, but he managed to stabilize before he took a tumble.

He reached the swing, and when he turned to sit down, his mommy and daddy were inside already.

Johnny stepped back and felt his weight shift into the seat of the swing. There weren't a lot of things that came natural to him, but swinging was one. He took another step backward to reach maximum height, and picked up his feet. He soared forward at a magnificent rate. Rising up, up, up to the sun. He wanted to reach for it again, but he had made a promise. He didn't want to upset his mother. He never wanted to see that look on her face again. He swung back and forth. The sun warmed his face. The wind tousled his hair.

Little three year-old Johnny leaned back, and closed his eyes. He gripped the ropes as tightly as he could. He made a promise. The rays of the sun lit up Johnny's eyelids each time the swing came forward. He saw red prints each time he felt the warm touch. Red, then dark. Red, then dark. Red, then dark. He could hear music. Calliope music.

The light sped up, and Johnny opened his eyes again. He was still sitting on the wolf, holding Harriet's hand. She was grinning like a fool, and so was he.

The calliope music wound faster and faster. The lights strobed faster and faster. Johnny and Harriet laughed loudly and held hands. The carousel spun faster. The centrifugal force began to push Johnny up off the wolf. He dropped Harriet's hand and grabbed the pole to stabilize himself. The lights flickered faster. Between the flashes the wolf changed. The fiberglass animals became skeletons, and in the blink of an eye changed back. Then the wolf became a dragon and turned back to face Johnny. Its snarling visage breathed hot smoke in his face. He laughed louder. Harriet's laughter joined his. The children on the ride laughed like people with screws loose. Johnny's hands slipped, and the belt that Harriet reminded him to fasten caught him. He repositioned himself around the pole. The carousel spun faster. Johnny looked at the tiger, which was no longer made of fiberglass. It swiped at him ripping his shirt and opening four long gashes on Johnny's chest. He wanted to scream in pain, but all that came out was a crazy laugh. All around him the children were losing their skin in the flashes of the lights. Johnny felt himself being lifted from the seat. He tried to call for Harriet, but his laughter wouldn't allow him to speak. None of this was right. He shouldn't be laughing. He was going mad. The children laughed. He could hear cicadas all around him. He couldn't stop laughing.

The ride slowed. Johnny sank back onto the seat. The lights flickered less violently. Then less. Then less, until they were the same yellow lights that were above him when they boarded the platform. All the noise fell off, except for the children's laughing, which sounded much more normal now. The dragon was gone. The tiger was gone. The only thing that remained was Johnny's frantic heartbeat. The calliope music warbled, then died off. The platform slowed, screeching to a halt. Johnny looked wildly at his wife. "What happened?"

"What do you mean?"

"What was that?" Johnny's mouth quivered. He looked at his shirt. The buttons were all there, and beneath it, his chest was smooth and dry.

"It was the carousel silly."

"Wha…" Johnny couldn't speak.

Harriet unbuckled his harness and, with his hand in hers, led Johnny to the ride's exit. "That was amazing," Harriet told the carney. She lifted Griz out of the bin and raced to the Ferris wheel.

"Wild ride, sir?" Larry said. "Careful out there. They's wild animals afoot."

4

Halfway there!

Ferris Wheel

Keep it going!

I'm sorry friend. I just been talking your head off. I bet your ears are fit to split.

No? Ha, you're being kind. But I like that. It shows you care. Business like ours, *entertainment*, it's good to know people still care.

I've been gabbin' an awful lot without asking you a thing: Tell me, what kind of show are you looking to put on in this theater of yours?

Oh of course, plays and musicals for the families. Yes, yes. Every theater does that. What's the hook though? What's going to put the butts in the seats? What's that thing you're not exactly coming right out and saying?

What's the secret?

Oh yes, I know P.T. Barnum. The man invented show business. *Flare.*

So you're saying you wanna put on a show with people flyin' around, and singin'?

You're gonna need quite the building for somethin' like that. A lot of space.

And you think the people of this town will want to see that? Even if it is during the week when the admittance would be cheaper?

Ha, you don't have to go no further. You had me at "folks from miles around."

I will say this, if you can fit in with the people in a small town, you can have whatever business you want.

And that can be said about anything you want to do. Not just business.

You got yourself an affinity for collecting wooden angels? All you gotta do is say it to one warm body, and in a day or two you'll have all the wooden angels you want. The problem is maintainin'. Everything can be going so perfect, so smoothly, and all it takes is one rub in the wrong direction to get the claws to come out.

You see, the small town ain't for everybody. For some people, small town life is only survivin' until you can get out. Even if it means becoming somethin' that deep down you ain't. I don't have to tell you one person it nearly chewed up and spit out.

It starts early. The weak are weak. The strong are strong. Survival. For Johnny it was junior high. That's where he met Rodney. When Johnny was in seventh grade, Rodney was a junior. By the time he was a senior, Johnny had caught up and would eventually surpass Rodney.

Every year there were less people between them on the adolescent food chain. Every year Rodney's focus pin-pricked a little more tightly around Johnny. After all, he was always scrawny and looked like such a dork with those glasses. Rodney made it his main concern to establish himself as the alpha male over Johnny, and the football team, and the teachers.

Arguably the greatest moment in Johnny's life was when he opened the letter, which he saw as a shining invitation out of the small town life.

I don't need to tell you at that point that his mother was already gone. There was an insurance policy taken out on her that became fully vested in Johnny's name on the day of his eighteenth birthday. Johnny used that money to buy a brand new, black Dodge Dart, and the rest went to the application fees for a number of different big-city schools.

Compared to Nowheresville, any school was part of a big city.

He wrote letters to a number of colleges, but there was really only one he wanted to attend. He received letters back from each of them offering full scholarships and multiple half scholarships for both his athletic and academic prowess. And he kept all those letters, every single one of them. He stacked them up in order of his preferences. The one he wanted to hear from of course was the last one to send a letter.

He walked into the post office every single day, hoping for anything resembling the royal purple lettering of the fabled Baton Rouge institution.

"Hey, Captain," he'd say to the retired army veteran behind the post office counter. "Did it come?" For weeks there was no good news.

When it finally did come, Johnny thanked Captain Boudreaux as calmly as he could. He pocketed the clean white envelope and fiercely pedaled his bike all the way down that dirt road leading to his house. He couldn't be bothered to set the kickstand up, and he just leaned the bike against the side of his house.

For a long while he didn't even open the letter. It was a thick letter, but they were all thick, so he didn't know if that was a good or bad thing. He couldn't steady his hands. He sat it on the kitchen table, and paced around it, and stared at it, and picked it up only to put it back down on the table. Every time he picked it up, he'd get a little closer to tearing it open before the tremble in his hands halted the process.

You see, these other schools were great. They had great programs, and they all had programs that Johnny wanted to attend. But none of them were in as big a city as Baton Rouge. Back then the population was nearly three hundred thousand. That's a number Johnny couldn't even fathom. Like I said, not everyone fits into a small town.

Leaving Nowheresville was more than just leaving people like Rodney and his lackeys and escaping the remnants from the aftermath of his mother. It was about the potential. The unknown. It was about having a choice for what to eat tonight. If he didn't like one pizza place, well he just went to the one down the street from that one. It meant life moved faster. If one store didn't have the right tool he needed, there was no need to wait three weeks for it to arrive. He just went to the store across town. It meant options. It meant having nearly three hundred thousand chances to have a legitimate connection with another person that didn't end with his head in a toilet or deflated tires and a long walk home.

When Johnny finally opened the letter, his arms were weak. They fell back to the tabletop and he dropped the letter face up. He read the purple and gold header to himself, blinking continuously because that was all he could do to keep from crying.

> Dear Mr. Jonathan Davis,
>
> Let me be the first to congratulate you on your admission status into Louisiana State University. We in the admissions office feel that with your academic history you will be a welcomed addition to our engineering department.

With the understood continuance of your academic achievements, we would like to offer you a full scholarship to our university.

We hope this letter reaches you in good spirits. If you are still interested in joining our community, please fill out and return the included copy of the scholarship request form. Welcome to LSU.

Sincerely,
Dean of Admissions

Below that there was a signature that Johnny wouldn't have been able to read even if he wasn't on the verge of hysterical tears. He started laughing. His body filled with uncontrollable excitement. He drummed on the table with his fists. Then that animal instinct of his kicked in. He huffed in breath to calm his laughter. When he was able to, he breathed deeply and let out a howl unlike any he had ever made.

AAAWWRRRROOOOO! OW! OW! OOOOOOWWWW!

The howl tapered off into a laugh, but a much more calm laugh than before. Howling is good for expelling a lot of energy all at once. Tears fell from his eyes onto the acceptance letter. He wiped them off and wiped his eyes with the collar of his shirt. It was the greatest moment of his life, until me of course.

He picked up the stack of papers and flipped the acceptance letter to the back. Behind it, instead of the scholarship request form he was expecting, there was another letter with the same purple and gold letterhead as the first. The only difference was that instead of the academic insignia, underneath the big bold "LSU" letters was the roaring head of a tiger. This one was from the Head of Sports Operations.

Dear Mr. Davis,

I wanted to congratulate you on your stellar performance in the Louisiana High School State Basketball Championship. Our head basketball coach was so thrilled with your performance that he personally spoke on your behalf to the admissions committee.

Needless to say, his efforts were greeted with support due to your academic history. Having said that, we would also like to offer you a full scholarship to play basketball at the guard position for the LSU Fighting Tigers through your senior year.

We understand that the academic scholarship you will receive will also be a full tuition scholarship. Should you choose to accept admission into our school, your athletic scholarship would cover your on-campus housing, as well as meals and give you a little extra each semester for other things you may need during your time as a Fighting Tiger. Welcome to the team.

Sincerely,
Head of Sports Operations

This was also followed by a scribbled signature that Johnny couldn't quite read. Johnny's animal instinct took over again and burst through his mouth, filling his house.

When the laughing stopped and Johnny felt as though the time had come to get serious, he flipped to the scholarship request forms. There at the top was that same purple and gold letterhead. Each form was accompanied by the insignia and logo that matched the department. He filled out the forms in less than two minutes. He sealed them both in a white envelope and tossed the stash of acceptance letters into the trashcan in the kitchen.

His dream had been realized. Johnny got to attend the biggest school in the area, following the dream of being educated and joining a division of the work force that showed no signs of ever slowing down. And because of the game he loved to play in the dirt patch in front of his house, he wouldn't have to get a job, distracting him from being the best at it. He couldn't wait to start packing everything he owned, which wasn't a lot. It'd only take one trip.

A funny thing happened to him then. A mild sense of unease washed over him, some deep longing to stay. Nothing powerful enough to hinder him from leaving Nowheresville, just enough to make him wonder what's out there. Like falling asleep to the faint sound of calliope music. It was as if something was holding onto him, but something weak. He took one more look at the sealed letter in his hand, and whatever it was released him. He never felt that again. From then on, it was all big city living for Johnny. Grocery shopping at nine o'clock at night. Buildings that blocked out the sun. Multiple streetlights throughout town. Everything was going green for Johnny Davis, future Jonathan Davis, doctor of mechanical engineering.

I know this takes you away from the story of how I acquired my most prized employee. There's a reason I tell you. Even in the saddest of lives, there are ups and downs. Backs and forths. And like a wheel we travel along the axis. Up and down, back to front.

This was the moment I wanted to take him. He was ridin' the five on the way to me, but he had something with him: hope. I couldn't take him yet. Hope is a very powerful thing. It can keep the most desperate alive for decades.

When I saw that black Dodge Dart scurrying up the five I couldn't even touch it. Neither could Harriet. So much energy in that car, no one could. He was ridin' high, my friend. If the radio wasn't fuzzy, he would've been singing at the top of his lungs. Didn't stop him for drumming on the wheel though. That time I had to just let him keep going. I knew I'd have my chance though. That was a down moment for Dandy D's Carnival Funland.

Ups and downs.

Backs and fronts.

Like a wheel.

Do you need a new drink, my friend? Gettin' low.

Just stop me if you get thirsty. Where was I?

Harriet ran, with Johnny struggling to keep up behind her. The children they passed pulled their parents in a similar way.

Johnny didn't know what to make of the things he had just seen. "Honey, can we slow down?" he asked. His voice bounced with each step he took.

"We gotta get in line!" Harriet called back.

If not for their joined hands, she would've left him at the carousel. Sweat rolled down the back of Johnny's neck and into his shirt. Beads of sweat like cold fingers tickled down his spine. His hair clung to his glasses, blocking his view on one side.

They reached the back of the line for the Ferris wheel. The sun had reached the point on the horizon where you could actually look in its direction without it hurting your eyes.

"The Ferris wheel has always been my favorite," Harriet explained.

"I know," Johnny said, but he didn't know how he knew.

"Honey, what's the matter?"

"I just... I," Johnny stammered. "I must've zoned out at the wrong time on the carousel."

"What do you mean?"

"You didn't see anything strange during the ride?"

"No, silly," Harriet laughed.

Johnny scoffed. "My eyes just had a weird moment, I

guess. The music and the lights went all crazy, it felt like it sped up, and I thought I was going to fly off of it."

"Are you sick, honey?" Harriet said, displaying genuine concern. "You look a little pale, and you're sweating."

"I feel strange."

"Do you think it was the food?"

"I didn't eat that much. And it was just the carousel. I know it's crazy," Johnny laughed. "But I swear I thought I saw the tiger you were riding come to life."

"All right, you must be seeing things, honey."

"I guess I got a little into the ride."

"You were howling like a wolf. I'm inclined to agree," she grinned at him sideways.

"You sure you didn't see anything?"

"I promise, I didn't," Harriet answered. "Here, let's open you up a little." She unbuttoned the top button of his shirt and vigorously fluffed the loose sides so the air would flow up and through the holes easier.

"You don't feel silly?"

"Of course I don't. Close your eyes."

"You're not going to put something weird in my mouth, are you?"

Harriet giggled. "Close them."

Johnny did.

"Put your arms up." Harriet pulled his arms over his head for him. "Keep'm there. Now breathe. Slowly."

Johnny did. Again. And again. He could smell the peppermint.

"Do you feel any better?"

"A little bit. Yeah."

"Do this for me." Harriet said. "Do you remember your first game?"

"For high school?"

"Yeah," Harriet said. This was one of the few organic memories she actually had of him. Something that was real. Something I didn't have to give her.

"Yeah, it was December. The weekend before Christmas."

"Tell me about it," Harriet said.

"You were there."

"I know, but I want to know your side of it."

"No. I mean *you* were there. That is my side of the story."

Harriet actually felt something, a warmth she hadn't felt in eleven years. It opened her. She blushed. "What else?"

"I remember feeling awkward in the blue uniform. I was used to wearing red and white. The team we always got beat by in elementary school was the Hornets and they wore blue and gold. It was more of a yellow than ours was, but they called it gold anyway. I remember feeling like I had betrayed my old team. But you were there. And you had your cheerleading uniform on. Seeing the blue and gold on your uniform, that made me feel like part of your team. Not theirs."

Unaccustomed to this feeling, to feeling anything at all, Harriet failed at fighting back the tears. A warm stream flowed through the place her heart had all but dried up. She wiped at the drops under her eyes and sniffled. Luckily for her, Johnny was obedient and kept his eyes closed.

I've done a lot of horrible things to get the people that I employ. I never rip them away from families, that's part of the reason I employ who I do, but I do rip them from their lives. I'm often distracted during my day by that very thought. But that's why the pinks are pinker, and the blues are bluer at Dandy D's. And in that poignant moment when tears slid onto Harriet's skin, I knew I had done the right thing by these two. It wasn't obvious to them, but it was to me.

"What else?" she whispered to hide the tremble.

Johnny lifted his head. "They were selling peanuts. I think that was the first time they did that. They had a fan by the concession stand that blew the smell all around the gym." Johnny grimaced. "That smell always grossed me out."

"You don't like peanuts?" Harriet laughed. Her face was wet.

"I don't like the smell. It's like oily or dirty. I don't know."

"You're so goofy," Harriet said. "They're letting people on, so I'm going to move you."

Johnny felt her pull his shirt and slid his feet across the metal ramp leading up to the loading platform.

"Keep going," Harriet said. She was under control of her voice again. Part of her didn't want to be.

"I remember thinking how much I wanted a root beer, but I knew I'd get a stitch in the middle of the game if I did. So I drank out of the cooler that had lukewarm water in it. You walked by me. You said, 'have a good game.'"

"I remember that," Harriet said.

"You said it to all the players."

"But I remember that one. You were the only kid on the team who was wearing glasses."

"Yeah," Johnny said. "I was the dorky one."

"I wanted to wear my glasses, but the cheerleading coach told me not to wear them. She said cheerleaders don't wear glasses."

"They told me that, too," Johnny said.

"And they let you play anyway?"

"I can't see without mine. If I can't see I can't make a shot."

"I wish I had spoken to you then."

"There were so many times I could say the same thing about you." Johnny felt the wind from the spinning wheel on his face. It felt the way the fan had, only now there was no dirty peanut smell. Just peppermint and bubblegum. "Mind if I open my eyes?"

Harriet wiped her face. "Go ahead."

Johnny did. His arms were still up, and the motion of the wheel carried his eyes upward. He felt like he had just released a three-point shot and was watching it sink into the net. Her hand slid from one of his shoulders to the other.

"I feel better," Johnny said, nodding his satisfaction.

"Me too," Harriet said. She curled up next to him to hide any remaining signs that she had cried for the first time in over a decade. "Tell me more about the game," Harriet said. She almost sounded timid. "I want to hear the rest. How'd you feel playing in the big time?"

Johnny laughed. "I don't think I'd say that exactly. I would hardly consider basketball at Nowheresville as playing in the 'big time.'"

"Yeah, but for the rest of them it was," Harriet said. And nothing she said about the Nowheresville student body was ever more exact.

You see, friend, Johnny entered that game barely on the roster. All the starters went on to work for the same construction company. For those boys on the team, that was the moment where they reigned supreme. The coach had told Johnny to practice a little without his glasses every day, and the better he got without them, the higher he would get on the playing chart.

Early in the first quarter, Donnie McAlister slid in sweat that wasn't toweled up and jerked his knee out of whack. And with that injury Johnny moved from the fifth guard on the playing chart, to the fourth. Then Johnny became less aware of the pretty girl across the gym, and more aware of the game being played between them.

The first quarter ended, and the starting guards had acquired a pair of fouls each. During the team huddle before the second quarter, Johnny listened to the coach telling the team to calm down. Play back. Watch the fouls. All of it was very appropriate for the starters, but what it sounded like to Johnny was, "Make sure Johnny doesn't get on the floor." He was at the back of the huddle, so it was easy to add one to the number of people listening to the cheerleaders.

The buzzer sounded, and the huddle broke. Nowheresville was on the bad side of the 16-12 score. The competitor in Johnny twisted an anxious knot in his stomach. Johnny concentrated his focus on the game, only taking the occasional glance at the cheerleader who stood on the end of the line.

Halfway through the second quarter the shooting guard racked up another foul. There had been no subs for the whole game so the coach put the number three guard in for the number two. The competitor in Johnny started warming up his legs. He was able to push sneaking glances at Harriet down to the number two priority.

Johnny kept his eye on the defender against whom he would be matched, number nine. He watched for weaknesses or patterns in his play. Number Nine was too conservative. When he went for a steal, he only went once. Even if the player Johnny would be replacing held the ball out with one hand in front of his face, Johnny didn't think he'd go in for a second chance.

Number Nine also played a little too close. That made him easy to shake off his guard. Johnny watched Number Nine for the remainder of the quarter. When the buzzer echoed through the gym signifying the end of the half, Johnny was more than ready to go into the game.

Nowheresville High didn't have any locker rooms. The visiting teams would go out a side exit and have their halftime meetings in the bus that brought them to campus. Johnny thought it would be better for privacy, and his attention, if the tigers left the building also. Instead, their halftime meetings were held underneath the home side bleachers.

The cheerleaders and the music from the speakers on the court kept the crowd loud enough to drown out the muffled speeches from below. You could only really hear them if you were lying on the bleachers with your ear positioned just right along the spaces between the boards. The only real downside was that Johnny's attention kept migrating to the view between the cracks. The view of the court. Of the cheerleader on the end of the line.

Even before he had a shot at ever being in the game, Johnny never actually heard the halftime speeches. But he saw the dance routine. When he talked to her—if he ever got the courage to just walk up to that cheerleader on the end and talk to her—he'd know just where to start. His first high school game was different though. The coach actually called on him.

"Davis," Coach said. "I want you in for Thompson here at the beginning of the half."

"Yes, coach." Johnny said quietly.

"What? Why?" Thompson argued.

"Because you been playing the whole game. You got three fouls on you already, and we can't afford to have you kicked out just because you ain't willing to sit for two minutes. Get your mind right, son. And if you get to thinking you got the onions to argue with me again, I'll make you a starter on the cheerleading squad, we clear?"

"Yeah," Thompson said.

"Yeah?" Coach answered.

"Yes sir, coach," Thompson corrected.

"Y'all, we ain't down by that much. Two or three unanswered, and we right back in this thing. We got Maxey, Davis, Phillips, Robins, and Clark in at the buzzer. Give me two minutes, and I'll get the starters back in there. Go shoot around so you can stay loose."

Two or three unanswered? Johnny thought. Had he been so focused on his own matchup that he didn't even know the score? Apparently, yes.

When the team came back onto the court, a cheer went up from the crowd. Johnny looked at the scoreboard and the home team was down twelve. An aggravated sigh left him as he took a ball from the metal rack and dribbled to the three-point line.

This is where he was comfortable. The ball rose over his head, and he let it fly. The net popped like a muffled firecracker.

"*Biiiiitch,*" a voice said.

Johnny begrudgingly turned to the voice. The ball came back to him and bounced off his chest.

"Way to go bitch!" Eli heckled.

"Make the shot!" Brett added.

The three of them clapped loudly and hollered ironic approval.

"Little *Biiiitch!*" Rodney called again.

Johnny saw an angry mother already making her way to the security guard whose current B-line ended right in the center of their trio.

"*Boys!*" the security guard shouted.

Rodney and his lackeys turned their attention to the oncoming storm. "Sorry, Mr. Parker," Rodney droned.

"You boys are going to watch your mouths," the meaty, red-faced security guard said through clinched teeth. "We have families here tonight, and y'all's bullcrap is not going to fly. Do you understand?"

"Yes, Mr. Parker," the three of them sing-songed.

"Y'all have a choice. Get your butts in seats, or hit the trail. What's it going to be?"

Unable to make any semblance of a decision for themselves, Eli and Brett deferred to their fearless leader.

"We'll get our butts in seats." Rodney laughed.

"Keep it quiet," Mr. Parker told them. "Y'all are going home if I have to say anything else in your direction."

The buzzer sounded as the three of them stomped loudly up the bleachers to the very highest seat. Johnny pushed them out of his mind.

The rest of the team jogged back to the bench leaving the second string on the court. Johnny shook away the jitters. There weren't any there, so it was all a show.

The whistle went up from the referee, and the away team's guards dribbled the ball down the court. Johnny homed in on Number Nine.

Number Nine was clearly winded from the first half. Their team only had eight players, so two starters had to be on the court at all times. Now that the Tigers were down to ten with Donnie McAlister's knee in the shop, Johnny began developing high hopes for the season.

Johnny gave Number Nine enough space to seem open. He was baiting his teammate into passing the ball. He took an extra step back. Number Nine called for the ball. Johnny watched while Number Six passed it around Johnny's teammate. He broke on the ball. This time when he tipped the pass, he was able to recover it. He stumbled with the ball, but the other guard broke and ran down the court. Johnny passed the ball ahead of him. His teammate sped up and caught the ball just in time to attempt a layup. The ball hit the underside of the rim and rebounded into the hands of the away team.

Johnny backpedaled and readied for defense. The ball never got close to him. After the short shot went through, Johnny jogged to the opposite end of the court waiting for the play call.

His teammate dribbled the ball down the court and called the same play from Johnny's freshman season.

Wait for the pick, curl, and get the ball.

He felt the pick from behind and spun behind it. The pass came, but it was behind Johnny. He had to readjust, and doing so brought an extra defender in his direction. Instead of forcing a bad shot, he passed the ball to his teammate around the defender. His teammate leapt up and sank an easy basket.

Finally some help.

There it was, the first offensive statistic of the season. He racked up an entire assist. Pah! I know one steal and one assist isn't much to warrant his own section of the crowd, but when the coach pulled him out at the first foul, he took Johnny to the side.

"Great job, buddy." Coach wrapped an arm around Johnny and talked quietly into his ear as if telling him a secret, but not one that had to stay that way. "Imagine if you got rid of them glasses. I'm gonna get you back in the game. Somewhere in the fourth. Get a seat. Way to play." Coach smacked him on his backside, the athletic equivalent of a punctuation mark at the end of a sentence.

Johnny took a seat on the bench and waited for the end of the quarter. The cheerleaders came onto the court to distract Johnny, and when they left, Johnny remained on the bench. The fourth quarter came and the seconds ticked off into minutes. Ten minutes left in the game became two, and the starting guard finally fouled out.

"Davis," Coach shouted. He waved Johnny over and wrapped his arm around him again. "We're too far down. Just make some points if you can. Come see me after the buzzer."

Johnny went in ten points down. The team lost, but Johnny helped close the gap. After each shot Johnny took, he left his shooting hand in the air until the ball touched the net. A sincere act of showmanship, but not over the top. Not distracting from the whole show. The game ended 68-64. Johnny's stat line for the game was much more impressive than his first outing as a freshman.

Shots M: 2, Shots A: 4 FTA: 1, FTM: 1, pts. 5, assist: 4, fouls: 1, steals: 2, blocks: 0

After the game, Johnny waited outside the gym alone on his bike. The lights went out, and Coach locked the gym once everyone had cleared out.

"Davis," he said startled. "I didn't see you there."

"Sorry, Coach," Johnny said. "It's dark out here."

"It's fine," he hesitated. "Listen, son. I may have been wrong for keeping you so low on the playing chart. I just know that those glasses are a bit of a liability."

"They're plastic," Johnny said. "They'll bend."

Coach chuckled. "Point is, I'm gonna have you a little higher from now on. You stay late all the time, and when you're in, you play your ass off. We need that on the team. I can't start you yet, but I'll sub you in more."

"Thanks, Coach."

"It's late, get on home."

Oh no. The dam.

A blade of worry cut through Johnny. The game wasn't too late, waiting for everyone to clear out was. Johnny was thankful for the darkness. The look on his face was embarrassing when he realized that his father would be waiting on the front porch for Johnny to get home.

Johnny stood on the pedals and didn't sit down until he was coasting up to the house. He saw Merle in the dirty orange light of the porch. Johnny parked his bike behind the house. The back door was locked.

The dam. I didn't rework the dam.

"Come on up here, boy." The voice beckoned him from the porch like a policeman.

Johnny would actually have preferred that. "Yes, sir," he called back. Johnny walked through the tall grass.

"Your mother ain't been here for ten years," Merle said. He was smoking one of his cigarettes. The revolver was sticking out of the top of his waistband. "When she was, you might get away with that. She cain't pick up after you now though. She cain't cover up for the shit you ain't doing."

Anger burned through Johnny.

"What did you forget to do?"

Johnny stopped at the bottom of the steps leading up to the porch. "Rework the dam."

"Why'd you forget to rework the dam?" Merle took the shovel that was leaning against the support pillar at the corner of the porch. "If you don't rework the dam, the well don't get filled. We ain't gone have water if water ain't in the well, boy."

"I know. I'm sorry."

"Sorry ain't what I asked for. Come here."

Johnny took one step up to the porch.

Merle swung the shovel. A large metal clang resounded in the open yard, followed by the thump of Johnny's weight on the ground of the dirt patch.

"Get out there and work the dam, boy."

He threw the shovel off the porch beside Johnny.

The sound of the metal in the dirt slowly raised pitch. It wasn't the sound of a shovel anymore. It was the sound of coins hitting the base of the Ferris wheel.

tinka tinka tink

Johnny was crying. He didn't realize he had been talking this long. The sound of children laughing eased him back to today.

"I didn't know that happened to you," Harriet said. Her eyes had dried, but her face showed obvious concern.

"Yeah," Johnny said, coming back to the present. "I'm sorry, I didn't mean to bring down your mood."

"No," Harriet said. She kissed him sweetly on the cheek. "It's really good to know more about you. I don't mind it at all."

"Have you been seeing things?"

"No, I'm fine."

"Nothing?"

"No, honey," Harriet wiped the lipstick off his cheek. "I really think it's just the food."

"Food never did that. I keep having these strange memories."

"Just don't think about it. Just be here with me."

"It's not that I'm remembering them. It's like I'm reliving them."

Harriet laughed. "Look at those kids. They're so small they can't even step into the ride. That's so cute."

At the head of the line there was a family of four. The parents were holding the two toddlers upright so they could make their own way onto the ride. The first was a little boy. His sister was bouncing behind him ready to "Go up high, like the monkeys in the cages. Right, mommy?" He was the younger of the two, and he dropped onto all fours to climb into the seat. The kid's diaper came down, and a little bit of baby bottom peaked out over the top.

Johnny laughed quietly.

"What's so funny?" Harriet asked. She grinned the way people do in the presence of a joke that hasn't been told yet.

"Do you remember Rodney Malone?"

"God, unfortunately." Harriet dramatically rolled her eyes.

"Do you remember the prank he played on the principal at the end of football season our junior year?"

"The paint one?"

"No, that was freshman year," Johnny corrected. "It was the paint one, then the sticky wax on his car seat, then the nails."

"Oh yeah, the nails. That nearly killed someone."

"Yeah, that was the one that got him expelled."

"What made you think about that?"

"The way that little kid just climbed onto the ride," Johnny laughed a little. "His pants came down, and his butt was showing."

"And that made you think of Rodney?"

"Well, yeah there was something about it that reminded me of the night he put the nails on the edge of the roof."

That night Johnny stayed in the gym until the janitors cleaned. He stayed on one side of the court while the janitor moved him closer and closer to the goal. He practiced three-pointers, then free throws, then rebounds, until there was no more uncleaned floor to use. He walked out of the gym with his own basketball in his hand. There was hardly any grip left. He'd have to use the money from Phil's to get a new one. The breeze cooled the sweat on his head. The air was wet with the pressure of an oncoming shower. He was about to take off his shirt and drop the ball in it so he wouldn't have to carry it on his bike when something on the roof made a loud thump. It was getting dark, and the noise startled him.

Johnny looked for what made the sound, but he didn't stop walking toward the bike.

"Eli, you numbnuts, just throw it up here."

"It's not heavy enough," Eli's voice was coming from the ground.

"Then tie the hammer to it, jackass," Rodney called out. "We need that up here anyway."

"Oh," Eli said, sounding as stupid as ever.

"What about the chain?" Brett called up.

"No," Rodney said, annoyed. "I told you the chain is to weigh down the fishing line."

"Oh," one of the two said. Johnny assumed it was Brett, but it sounded equally as dumb as the one before it.

"Hang on," Rodney said quietly. "I heard someone."

Johnny ran back underneath the awning above the gym door. He held his breath and stood as still as he possibly could. He couldn't see the roof from where he stood, but when Rodney peered over the edge, Johnny could tell Rodney was looking for him. He could feel his presence. Johnny stiffened.

"Hey!" Rodney barked.

His footsteps clomped away.

Johnny deflated. He peeled away from the gym door.

Johnny crept around the building to see what the lackeys were doing.

"Give me the nails, hurry," Rodney shouted.

That was enough for Johnny to retreat. Johnny didn't want to be part of what Rodney had planned, especially if it required nails.

There was a metallic bang on the roof. Johnny jumped again, almost screamed. He ran through the grass to his bike. It was quieter than stomping up the walkway that connected the gym to the school, but not quiet enough.

"You hear that?"

Johnny jumped back onto the walkway pretending not to hear them. He reached his bike just as Rodney dropped from the roof to the awning.

Rodney got on his hands and knees to ease himself over the side of the awning. When he bent down his pants fell halfway to his thighs. His ass gave the world a show, but Johnny was the only person in the audience.

"Shit," Johnny whispered as Rodney ran up to him.

"Hey, little bitch. Where you going?"

"Just going home, Rodney," Johnny said, playing ignorant.

"What'd you see, bitch?"

"I just left the gym. I didn't even know you were here."

"We're just doing a prank."

"Well, thanks for letting me know. I'll be able to avoid it."

"Better keep your fucking mouth shut."

"I didn't even see anything," Johnny climbed on his bike. He started to pedal away. "I wouldn't even know what to say."

Rodney grabbed the handle bar and jerked Johnny nearly to the ground. The basketball fell out from under Johnny's arm. "Here's what we're doing then."

"No, Rodney. Seriously."

"We're tying a bucket of nails to a chain, and rigging it to fall when the security guard picks it up."

"Why?"

"Every time we go to a game he has some bullshit to say to us."

"Well, you do tend to invite that," Johnny said.

"He's gonna stop riding our asses after this."

"You could really hurt him; you do understand that, right?"

"That's the point."

"I don't understand why you're even telling me this."

"Because if you know," Rodney finally let go of the handlebar. "That makes you part of it. If we get caught, we'll say you knew the whole time. You'll go down, too." Rodney snatched the ball off the ground. He pulled a screwdriver from his pocket and stabbed it into the ball. He laughed like a mad hatter. Not because it was funny, but because it got to Johnny when he did. "Goodnight, little bitch." Rodney ran around the building, continuing his lunatic laugh, and watching Johnny over his shoulder.

"I made it home before it was completely dark," Johnny told Harriet as they stepped forward with the flow of the line waiting to get on the Ferris wheel. "I wanted to wake up early and set it off or disarm it. Whatever you call it. The janitor went out that door when he finally left. He always parked behind the gym because that's where his day's work ended. And there weren't any closets to keep the mop like at the school building, so he just left it in his truck. When I got there, he was on the ground, unconscious. I felt like it was my fault. It was."

"It wasn't though," Harriet slid her hand in his. "It was Rodney's. If you had gone back he would've hurt you. You tried. That's what matters."

"The principal was already there. He was always there before anyone else. I went to his office and told him everything I saw. Everything I knew. He called the sheriff. Twenty minutes later, the janitor was in the hospital. Three weeks after that he was back in the gym waiting for me to finish practicing. He never thanked or condemned me. I always wished he would've done one or the other. I never knew what language he spoke. I just knew I didn't speak it. That's why I never apologized. The one time I tried he just looked at me like there were ants on my face."

They were quiet for a moment.

"It's amazing to me that he gets to just walk around with normal people."

"He's lucky to be alive," Johnny said, staring up to the top of the wheel. "There was a lot of carnage that morning behind the gym."

"I was talking about Rodney."

"I know," Johnny said, grinning at her. "I was trying to break the tension with a joke."

Harriet laughed quietly, shaking her head. "Think we'll have to wait another round?"

Johnny looked up to the front of the line. The carney wasn't the one from the game or the ride. He couldn't tell if he was relieved or not. Deep down he knew that somehow they'd get on this round. Everything seemed to break their way today. He shrugged anyway. Not for him, for her. Constantly putting on a show, that Johnny. "I don't know. Looks hopeful though."

The line crept forward. One by one the bench seats were filled, and the wheel would move around to allow more to be filled. Johnny counted the seats that were left to be filled and guessed that they would be the first ones for the next round. He recounted, starting with the bottom where the new carney stood. There were three groups of people left to board the ride, and Johnny counted 1, 2, and 3 benches left to fill. The ride naturally drew his eyes upward, and when his line of sight circled back down, there was a familiar face waving him forward.

"Hey," Larry said. "You there, the happy couple."

"Us?" Harriet said.

"Yeah, you two," Larry said. His uniform was now purple and white. "The happy couple. Come on. These people said they'd like to trade places with you. Got'a sick passenger."

Johnny looked suspiciously at Larry.

Harriet said, "Oh, no. Are you not feeling well, little guy?"

"My tummy hurts," the little boy said. His sorrowful voice saved him the effort of saying, Oh woe is me!

"I hope you feel better, little darling," Harriet said, tousling his hair. She dropped Griz in a similar prize storage crate that was waiting at the end of the line for the carousel.

"Yeah," Johnny said. His mind reached for justification,

anything that would explain why everything was breaking his way today. Then the smell of Harriet's gum and peppermint lured him onto the Ferris wheel. "Feel better, buddy, okay?"

Harriet sat on the bench and tapped the seat beside her with her hand. "Join me?"

Johnny bowed, "Why, yes, my lady."

As Johnny sat beside her, Larry fastened the chain on the side of the bench from the front to the back. "Don't want you to fall out," Larry chuckled. "You two have fun."

"We'll try," Johnny said. "I hear they's wild animals afoot."

"Ezzactly," Larry said. He winked at Johnny.

It didn't settle Johnny the way it could've been perceived to do. It wasn't the tongue-in-cheek acknowledgement of a joke. It felt like a warning. Johnny didn't have a chance to say anything before the ride began to move.

But he wasn't standing anywhere near the controls.

"Thank you for riding this with me," Harriet said. "I know it's pretty childish, but I love being up high. It's the best view of the city, even though it doesn't really face the city."

"What does it face?"

"The hill," Harriet said. Her voice was hypnotizing. It rolled out of her like the current flowing down a creek. "It's where the city gets the name."

"You mean Nowheresville?"

"This isn't Nowheresville," Harriet said. "This is Rose Colline."

"What haven't I even heard of it?"

"It's a small town," Harriet said. "Maybe a little bigger than Nowheresville, but it's not like anything happens of interest to the people here let alone to people in other small towns."

Johnny considered this. "Yeah, that makes sense."

"Rose Colline is French for 'Pink Hill.' From the top of the wheel you can see the hill."

"It's a pink hill?"

"There's a plant that grows on it called muhly grass." Her voice changed slightly then. She allowed a bit of excitement to creep in. "This is the perfect time of day to ride the Ferris wheel. The sunset blends the colors together, and you can't really see the green of the stems. It's totally pink."

The wheel slowed as Johnny and Harriet reached the pinnacle of its rotation.

"I can see it," Johnny said. The hill was completely pink. The breeze blew the tops of the plants in waves. The motion of the field created the illusion of the tide washing up on a grassy shore. In the center of the hill, an oak tree stood tall with its branches reaching down to the pink hill. The way the sunset shined on the branches gave the leaves the look of fire. Johnny could almost smell smoke. Then the sun set, leaving the hill in darkness. It happened too quickly, but with everything he had seen today, Johnny didn't bother saying anything. Probably just a trick his eyes were playing on him.

"It's beautiful," Harriet said. "That's why I never want to leave. It takes me away. All I have to do is get on the wheel, and I can see myself on those waves. Those waves can be anything. An ocean washing up on a beach. The sheets on a bed fluttering in the wind from an open window. A pink field in the middle of nowhere. We don't have to feel alone."

"Do you feel alone?"

"Not with you," Harriet said. Her fingers slipped between Johnny's.

"Is this place—" Johnny began.

But then something happened.

The wheel started upward.

We were at the top.

"What's happening," Johnny asked. He looked around for some kind of clarification. His hands wrapped around the bar in front of him.

"We're just going up," Harriet said.

"We were at the top." Johnny was starting to panic.

"Hey, hey," Harriet said. Her hand slipped around his arm. "It's fine. It's just a ride."

"I just don't like heights," Johnny said. He leaned back next to Harriet. "When I get up too high, my vertigo kicks in, and I start feeling strange."

"It's just a ride," Harriet repeated.

They were so high up that the carnival lights began to fade from view. The bench seat swayed, and Johnny shouted with fright.

"Sorry," Johnny said, beginning to laugh. His hand gripped the bar "I don't know what's wrong with me."

Harriet began to laugh with him. "You're just being silly,

sweetheart. Let go. Have fun."

The ride jerked upward. The force coming down on the pit of Johnny's stomach threatened to send everything out. Being up this high made him lightheaded. The bench came to a stop just as the light ran out. Johnny saw the bluish hue of Harriet's face in the moonlight and little else. He knew how high up they were, but he couldn't see anything around him. His balance shifted beneath him. He groaned to fight off the nauseated feeling in his stomach.

"How are you feeling, honey?" Harriet's voice came to him from far away.

Neither of them could stop laughing.

The bench tilted forward, but that wasn't all. The Ferris wheel leaned. At first it felt like only an inch back and forth, and Johnny just thought it was the vertigo. He blinked away the feeling. The bench seat tipped forward even more. The sway became more noticeable. What was only an inch became a foot, then two. Johnny latched onto the safety bar to steady himself.

Then the bench dropped.

Johnny felt his weight lift off the bench. The ride tipped toward Harriet's side of the bench. They fell so fast that if not for the chain blocking their exit, Johnny would've been thrown clear of the Ferris wheel.

Harriet laughed. He laughed. They couldn't stop. Because at Johnny D's Carnival Funland no one goes home unhappy.

The bench lifted again the way a metronome returns to the opposite side of the stand. Johnny pulled Harriet to him.

She squeezed him tightly. He felt her breath on his neck. As the bench descended again, the light from the carnival illuminated the bench, and when Johnny met Harriet's eyes, a deep gash had been carved out of her face. It ran from the right corner of her mouth into her hairline. Johnny's stomach turned at the sight of the white bone of her skull. She was missing teeth, and the skin around her eye sagged.

As the Ferris wheel stopped tilting, the sweat on Johnny's hands loosened his grip on the safety bar. He fell toward the bench's exit. The chain caught around the gut and snapped. Johnny was slowed just enough to regain control on the hold he had on the safety bar.

"Harriet!" he shouted through his hysterical laughter.

"Johnny!" she gleefully replied.

The wheel rebounded upward and came to an abrupt stop hundreds of feet above the carnival. Johnny was thrown onto Harriet's side of the bench, pinning her against the barrier between them and a plunge to certain death.

"That was so much fun!" Harriet whispered to him. The wound on her face was gone. When she smiled, all her teeth were present. She put her hands on each side of his face and pulled him to her for a kiss. Johnny calmed considerably.

"What just happened?" Johnny asked. His heart was racing, but he couldn't form an answer for why.

It was just the Ferris wheel. Your vertigo kicked in, and you got all loopy.

"We rode the Ferris wheel!"

The wheel turned, bringing the happy couple slowly to the ground. Sweat cooled Johnny's face. Johnny felt the way he imagined he felt as a toddler when his mother tossed him in the air, caught him, and eased him safely back onto the ground. When their bench reached the platform, Larry was there to undo the chain still protecting them from falling out of the seat.

"Have fun?" Larry asked, smiling at them sideways.

"That was so much fun," Harriet said as the happy couple disembarked the wheel.

"Feeling all right, sir?"

"I have a thing about heights," Johnny said.

"Well, you're back on land now, and since you two are the happiest couple of folks I've seen all night, I'll give you one of these." Larry handed Johnny a coupon: Meal for 2 Any stand in the joint.

"You're just giving us a free meal?" Johnny asked.

"Well, of course," Larry said. "I get one of those a day, and you two…nobody deserves one more than the two of you. Enjoy. The hotdogs are the best in the world."

"Will do," Johnny said, putting the coupon in his shirt pocket. He offered Harriet his hand.

"Thank you, honey," she said, taking his hand and stepping back onto the platform. "That's perfect timing. I'm starving."

"See you later," Larry said.

"Careful out there," Johnny said.

"Wild animals," Larry said. He winked. "I'm on it."

5
Tilt-a-Whirl

Johnny reluctantly used the coupon in his front pocket to get a corndog and soda for him and Harriet. He was growing suspicious of the preferential treatment. Luckily, everything was going exactly the way we expected.

"These things are enormous." Johnny handed Harriet a corndog with mustard and ketchup slathered on either side. When she took it, he handed her a soda from the crook of his arm.

"Good," Harriet said. She licked her lips. "I'm starving. I may even go back for seconds."

"That's like a pound of meat and bread," Johnny said.

"Maybe even two," Harriet said. She held the dog in front of her face, and to Johnny's surprise, it actually hid her.

"That's a mess." Johnny sat across from her and Griz at one of the picnic tables between the Ferris wheel and Wacky

Walter's Concert Bonanza stage. Wacky Walter had just kicked off the first performance of the night.

"I like that they put the ketchup and mustard right on the outside of the corndog," Harriet said. "It's like they know most people are going to keep on walking around so instead of giving them something extra to carry for dipping, they just plop it right there on the side of the corndog. Saves a whole step in the corndog process. Brilliant."

"I'm glad you're enjoying the condiment delivery method."

"I am," Harriet said. She took a bite out of the dog.

Johnny noticed she didn't take the gum out of her mouth first. "Are you not eating peppermint?"

"No, I'm eating a corn dog."

"But you smell like peppermint and bubblegum. You always do. I just assumed you were eating one of the two."

"Oh, I usually do," Harriet said. "The peppermint keeps me calm."

"Does it work?"

"I'm pretty calm."

"So, then why do you chew gum, too?"

"Because I don't like the taste of peppermint," Harriet said.

Johnny laughed. "And I don't like the smell of peanuts."

"Exactly," Harriet said. There was a rare silence in the conversation. With a full mouth of corndog, Harriet said, "What's the matter, sweetheart?"

"I'm fine."

"You sure?" she asked. "You're not worried about feeling sick, are you?"

"No, it's not that."

"Because that may have been because we haven't eaten all day. You know what hunger can do to a person. I bet this will help."

"I bet it will."

"So, what's the matter then?"

Johnny paused, translating his thoughts into words that might explain them. "Do you think it's strange that we haven't spent any money since we got here?"

"What?" Harriet asked in shocked disbelief. "No, that's impossible."

"No, I'm serious."

"That can't be. There's an entrance fee just to get inside."

"But the clown guy didn't charge us, remember?" Johnny said. "He said he couldn't charge a happy couple like us."

"That's doesn't sound right."

"And the bear," Johnny pointed to Griz. "He said I could shoot until I missed."

"He charged you a penny to do it, though."

"Well, he said it would be a penny. He even made a point to shake his cup at me, but still, he never took the penny."

"Are you sure?"

"I'm positive," Johnny said. "And this food. The Ferris wheel carney, who by the way is the same guy as all the rest of them, just gave us a coupon?"

"Are you mad about it?"

"No," Johnny said. He realized that he was peering not

just in the mouth, but also down the throat of the gift horse. "It feels weird. I mean we don't even know these people. Do we?"

Harriet paused. She chewed her mouthful of corndog. "No."

"I don't know anyone here," Johnny said. He looked around for anyone he knew.

"Sweetheart, it's just our day," Harriet said. "Some people never even get a moment that's theirs. Yeah some people strike gold on the stock market or whatever, and some people become president. Ours just happens to be the small town version of that. It felt good being the center of attention when you were playing that basketball game, didn't it?"

"Yeah, it did," Johnny answered.

"And it melted my heart to—"

Feel something.

"—to have you win that bear for me," Harriet finished. "This just happens to be our day."

"I guess you're right."

"So let's enjoy it."

"Did you feel like you were going to fall out of the Ferris wheel?"

"No," Harriet said. "I felt fine. Did you?"

"Maybe it was the colors or something. I really thought I was going to fall out."

"Was it your vertigo?"

"It's never been that bad. I thought we went so high that we couldn't see the lights anymore. And the sunset was strange. Too fast or something."

"I mean we did get to ride for longer than usual. I guess the carney just thought we'd appreciate a little alone time away from the young'n." Harriet tipped her head to Griz.

"I bet that's it," Johnny said, smiling at his wife.

They leaned over the table toward each other and shared a kiss over their sodas. They sat back down and continued eating.

"Thank you for stopping," Harriet said.

"It wasn't a problem," Johnny said. "It was a bad day, and I think it made both of us feel better to stop and have a little fun."

"That's true," Harriet said. Then remembering that feeling she had earlier, she asked, "Do you think you could tell me about another one of your basketball games?"

"You want to hear about another game?"

"Yeah," she said. "Didn't we win the state championship?"

"We did," he said. "I remember seeing the banner in the gym at the reunion. They had the welcome sign blocking it. I don't know why, but when I saw that, I wanted to tear it down."

"I think it's because you saw that as the high school trying to cover up the one thing you enjoyed doing there. Like they were trying to forget you were good at something."

"Maybe you're right." Johnny considered that for a second, and the more he did, the more he agreed with it. "The game was against Slidell. They didn't do it the way they do now where it's in Baton Rouge regardless of who plays. The team with the better record got the home court advantage, and we only lost one game that year. The first game of the season."

"Were you playing?"

"Yeah, but I was rusty I guess. I wasn't used to having someone to pass the ball to. Coming back as the one starter who wasn't invited to practice with everyone else over the summer was a hard thing to catch up with. Sometimes it was like they forgot I was there. I had it down by the second game though. In the championship, we were playing the team that won it all the year before. They were the Cyclones. We almost played them, but we lost the regional round.

"I played almost the whole game. I don't know if you remember this, but my first game ever I only got to play for about two minutes. I scored two points on free throws because someone had to come out for a break. By the time I was a starter, I was the guy that only came out for an occasional rest. Were you there? I usually remember you when I think about basketball games. You were the only cheerleader I even saw."

"I think I was," Harriet said. She knew she wasn't. By then she would've been a part of the Dandy D's family. "I was at all the games. I had to be for cheerleading."

"You sure? I guess I had my head too far into the game. That whole season was kind of a blur. I remember being sore though. I can't think of why. I had a bruise on my back. My neck was stiff. I think I wrecked my bike or something. I stretched a lot before that game."

And deep down Johnny knew that no matter how much

he stretched before tipoff, his back would feel the same way. He mostly did it to look like a basketball player. There were scouts from every college to which he planned to apply, including one in a royal purple polo at the top of the bleachers all the way across the gym from the home team's bench. He wanted to look like he cared. Even to the naked eye of a layman, it was clear that the Davis kid cared.

Johnny had that game won before the visiting team even got off the bus. He was sore from top to bottom from what Rodney had done to him, and that was a couple weeks before championship weekend. Johnny wondered why, even as they faded from his skin, no one asked where he got the bruises. Not even Coach.

It started at tipoff. The ball fell right in his hands. He passed it to the point guard and set up in formation. The guard called the play. Pick and roll. The team had run that play hundreds of times between his first game and his last. They had even run it successfully dozens of times in games, but this was championship. It had to be perfect. Johnny felt for the pick. When it came he faked inside, planted his foot, and spun around his help. The defender tripped over his own feet, tumbling through the pick, and taking out a teammate in the process. The pass came down the midway with a single bounce. Johnny caught it in stride, and without dribbling, he made the layup. He didn't smile. He didn't flaunt in any way. He only applauded and jogged to his place in the defensive formation. He was the only player on his team who wasn't standing straight up.

The game continued in his favor. By the sound of the

halftime buzzer, Johnny had racked up two steals, four assists, and twelve points. He had even made a pair of three-pointers. During the halftime rundown from Coach, Johnny was completely focused. There was no sneaking glances through the cracks in the bleachers. There was no pining over the pretty girl on the end of the cheerleaders' line. He was in basketball mode and had been the entire season. Being a starter from the beginning changed the way Johnny played the game.

"Davis," Coach said. "We gonna rest you for a few minutes. Go ahead and go shoot around. We ain't gonna win if you go cooling off."

"Got it, Coach."

Johnny walked out from beneath the bleachers.

"Little bitch," Rodney said. The lackeys cackled in their typical chimp-like cavorting. It was like Johnny had his own cheering section.

Johnny ignored him. He walked to the team cooler and filled a paper cup. He downed the water on the way to the trashcan at the end of the bench. He tossed the cup, and picked up the ball next to it. He stepped onto the court, just barely inbounds. He raised the ball over his head, and let it fly. His hand stayed in the air, for the sake of showmanship of course, until the net whipped up. Johnny waited for the chorus of lackeys to sing behind him. Nothing happened. He wanted to make sure they were still alive, but he correctly assumed their attention had shifted to a younger prey than him. He jogged up to the ball, tipped in a quick short shot, and moved back to the three-point line. He dribbled once, shaking an imaginary defender, and let the ball fly. The net snapped up just like before. Johnny dropped his hand.

The rest of his team filed out from beneath the bleachers, and Johnny resolved himself to the position of rebounder. He passed the balls to the players who would be starting the second half. He was a real team player. The scoreboard had them ahead thirty-two to twenty-five. Johnny had only one foul, and so far no one had fouled him. Almost like people were avoiding the bruises underneath his jersey.

The buzzer honked. Johnny took his spot on the bench. The smell of peanuts tormented him. He missed the smell of peppermint and bubblegum in the gym. His junior season he would deliberately travel to the cheerleaders' side of the court to drown out the peanuts. He didn't do that as a senior. He had no interest in the cheerleaders as a senior. Johnny focused on the game.

The minutes ticked off the clock. The score barely changed, but the Cyclones had managed to close the gap. Six minutes had ticked off the third quarter before Coach decided to put Johnny back in the game. The thought was if they lost the game with the starters on the bench for more than half a quarter, he'd be the only one to blame. He called time out.

The team huddled around him. Johnny remained on the outside.

"Maxey, Davis, Pitts, Turner, and Butler," Coach began. "Get back in there and finish this thing. We're only down by three. Nothing we can't handle. Start with the pick and roll."

"Coach, we need to switch," Turner said. He was gesturing to Pitts. "His guy is too aggressive. He's a better shooter. He'll free up easier."

"That's fine. It's thirty-nine to thirty-six. We need to be tied by the end of three. Got it?"

"Got it," the starters answered.

"Get out there," Coach said. "We ain't going home without the trophy."

The whistles blew, and the game continued with all the starters on both teams.

The second attempt at the pick and roll gave Johnny another assist.

By the time the buzzer sounded, declaring an end to the third quarter, the Tigers were back on top. It was forty-six to forty-two. The team huddled back up.

"Who hasn't played?" Coach asked. Two players raised their hands. One was a guard, and the other was a forward. "Shit, why ain't you say somethin'? Damnit. Okay, I'm sorry, guys. Blakeney and Kelly go in. Davis and Pitts, give them two minutes."

Anger burned in Johnny. He felt like his stomach had been branded.

"Two minutes," Coach pleaded. "Two minutes and you two will be back in."

"It's fine," Johnny said. He silenced the rage by concentrating on the idea that he was also given a chance that lasted two minutes. Kelly was a lot like him, so Johnny didn't mind helping someone the way Coach helped him four seasons ago. Johnny got some water and took a seat at the end of the bench. The buzzer honked again to round up the players for the final quarter. Johnny watched the scoreboard nervously.

"You'll be right back out there," Coach said.

Johnny jumped. The cheering from the stands gave Coach a little more stealth than usual. "It's fine, I get it. They may not get to play in the championship again."

"You're a good kid, Johnny," Coach said, smacking him on the back. "Let me talk to Pitts. He ain't taking it as well."

In two minutes the Tigers had relinquished four turnovers and came back down the scoreboard. The score was fifty to forty-eight.

"Davis, Pitts," Coach called. "Get back in there."

Johnny leapt off the bench and jogged out to his position on defense. The starters held the team to a scoreless possession. Johnny sprinted down the court and stopped at the three-point line. He raised his hands for a pass. Pitts bounced it across the court and readied for defense. Johnny caught the pass after the second bounce, turned to the goal and shot the ball. His hand stayed in the air even after the net snapped like a whip. Johnny backpedaled to his position on defense.

Back in the lead. Much better.

The crowd roared.

Johnny's demeanor was cold. Ready for anything. Having the lead late in the game meant there was nothing to worry about. The minutes ticked away into history. With only two left, the tigers were up by six. The Cyclones were purposely fouling in hopes of the Tigers missing free throws.

The game slowed as if being dragged behind a mule, just like it always did in the last minutes. There were always two guarding Johnny. Any time one of his teammates got the ball they were immediately fouled. Johnny only got the ball once, and the Cyclones swarmed him. There were four people around him. They had planted their feet and raised their arms high taking away any chance of Johnny making a shot. Johnny passed to Pitts, who was immediately fouled by the one remaining defender. Pitts made one shot and missed the other. The Cyclones struggled to even pass half court on the next possession. Johnny's stat line read:

Shots M: 8, Shots A: 13 FTA: 0, FTM: 0, pts. 20, assist: 9, fouls: 1, steals: 4, blocks: 0

The game ended sixty-four to fifty-nine. The fans rushed the court slinging their drinks and popcorn and peanuts everywhere. A mob of people collected around the starting Tigers, and Coach cheered. There were high fives and hugs for everyone. The state league official pushed through the mass and presented Coach with the state championship trophy. It was doused in soda and flakes of peanut shells. The team lifted Coach on their shoulders and bounced him in the air.

"I was on the outside of that huddle, too," Johnny told Harriet. "That was all right with me. Coach always smelled like cigars and wood."

"He did," Harriet laughed. There was a pause from her. She processed the uncomfortable feeling of being left out of something in which she was supposed to take part. "That was a great night, wasn't it?"

"It was," Johnny agreed. "I never understood why no one fouled me until today. They thought it was more likely that I'd miss a shot being guarded than miss either of the two free throws fouling me would bring."

"You were great," Harriet said.

"I wasn't even the best on the team. Pitts had almost thirty points that game. Five blocks, too. People love blocked shots on defense."

"He was a lot taller," Harriet said. "I'd rather have you on my team. Even if it isn't basketball." Harriet looked at the thin watch around her wrist and glanced at the sky, which was now black with the exception of a few scattered specks of light. She chewed the remaining crust off the stick. She took a long drink out of her soda and wiped her mouth with one of the napkins that came with the dog. She turned her attention back to Johnny.

"Wow," Johnny exclaimed. "You just put that entire corndog away."

"Would you excuse me?"

"Absolutely," Johnny said. "You want seconds?"

"No," Harriet said. She gathered the trash. "I just have to take care of something."

"Oh, restroom," Johnny said quietly. He nodded in an understanding gesture.

"Sure," Harriet laughed. She walked around the picnic table, sliding her hand up his arm as she passed him. "Watch Griz for me?"

"He'll be fine. I'm a good parent." Johnny bit into his

corndog. Mustard dripped onto his white shirt. He turned in the direction where Harriet walked. "Oh, can you get me a…" He trailed off when he couldn't find her. He looked at Griz peering at him over the table then back to the stand with the napkins. "No big deal. Be right back, Griz." He didn't even feel silly saying it. Johnny left Griz at the table and retrieved a couple napkins to handle the stain. He looked over Griz's shoulder and saw a sign for the public restrooms.

"So now that we've eaten," Harriet started. She was walking back from behind him. She carried a different smell with her. That smell was still there, but there was a faint tinge of cigarette smoke. It didn't overpower the peppermint, but it was there, like a stain at the bottom of a dress. "And we've ridden the classics. So what do you want to do now?"

"I know this may be a questionable decision after eating deep fried bread and meat, but I've never been on the tilt-a-whirl. You up for that?"

"No!" Harriet said, feigning shock. "Well, come on. Let's go."

Harriet snatched Griz off the picnic table seat and pulled Johnny toward the tilt-a-whirl.

As they hurried down the midway to the ride, Johnny's stomach felt fine. There was no stitch, no nausea, nothing. Maybe the corndog and soda was exactly what he needed. Sometimes all you need is something disgusting to make you feel better. They passed a number of barkers for games and rides. None of them looked anything like Larry.

"Win the lady another prize?" a high striker carney tempted. He also wasn't Larry. Johnny was almost let down. He had gotten used to seeing that familiar face everywhere they went. "Smack the lever, hit the bell, win the prize. Simple, simple!"

"We'll come back," Johnny said. Harriet pulled him along. "We're late for a ride."

The line for the tilt-a-whirl was short. Even without their presidential treatment, they'd be riding the next round.

"The tilt-a-whirl is great!" Harriet said. "It's a like a thrill ride that never leaves the ground. You're gonna get so dizzy!"

"Have you been here before?"

"Oh, yeah," Harriet said. "Everyone comes to Dandy D's. Have you?"

"I came here with my parents when I was a kid."

"It's fun, right?"

"I honestly don't remember." He did remember that day with the ice cream, but nothing that happened after that. He watched the ride. Red, white, and blue-striped saucers with people inside spinning. He'd never seen this ride in person. He didn't know what to expect. "So what's the deal with this?"

"Okay," Harriet said. Her excitement was pouring out of her. "So you and I sit in the little eggshell things. There will be a round table-like thing on the inside. That's how we'll control the eggshell."

"We control the ride?"

"Yeah!" Harriet continued. "Everyone goes in the big

circles around the track. But the eggshells are suspended so you can spin even more. The trick is you gotta spin it as hard as you can."

"So basically we can go faster than anyone else."

"Competitive, huh?" Harriet said, smiling. "If you want to go fast, we'll spin like a tornado. I think it's slowing down."

The motor that controlled the ride slowed then. A loud decelerating sound growled up from beneath the platform.

"Good call," Johnny said.

Johnny started to slip from our influence. Harriet grabbed his hand. "This is going to be so much fun."

The ride came to a stop. People stampeded for the exit, giggling and shouting about where they were going next.

"Where do you want to go next?" Johnny asked.

Harriet pretended to think. "We should go to the haunted house."

"Is it scary?" Johnny asked pretending to be afraid.

"It's really scary," Harriet said. "It scared me to death."

There was something in her voice that caused something to grip Johnny's stomach and squeeze. "You're kidding."

"Yeah, I'm kidding," Harriet giggled. "I'm here, ain't I?"

The line began to move. There were only two groups of teenagers and two families ahead of them. Harriet led Johnny to an empty eggshell.

"Have fun, you two," Larry said. His suit was red this time.

They sat down with Griz between them. There was a padded bar that lowered into their laps for safety. The walls of the eggshell were black. It felt familiar.

"Watch this." Harriet grabbed the wide circle and pulled. The eggshell slowly turned.

"Wow," Johnny said. "It's that easy?"

"Pretty cool, right?" Harriet said. She was really selling it. "If you keep the momentum going, the ride gets that much better."

The motor underneath the platform roared back to life.

"Here we go," Harriet said, beaming.

The platform began to spin.

Something startled Johnny. A memory. He shouted as if something pinched him.

"Honey, what's wrong?" Harriet asked. This was the first time she wasn't expecting a reaction to the ride.

"I just remembered something," Johnny said. "It's nothing. Let's spin."

"Spin!" Harriet shouted.

They grabbed the edge of the table and pulled. The eggshell spun counterclockwise on the platform. The laughter began. The lights on the platform changed from white to green and pink. It created an oily atmosphere.

A feeling of déjà vu came to Johnny. Not because he had been here before, but because he had felt this same sensation of uncontrollable spinning in a dark, enclosed place.

"Spin!" Harriet repeated.

"Spin!" Johnny said. "Faster!"

Johnny closed his eyes, and the memory flooded him.

He was at Phil's. It was closing time. Johnny was sweeping, but more than that he was watching the cheerleaders and football players at the table outside. They had just lost in the regional round of the playoffs.

Been there, guys. Johnny thought.

They weren't the usual upbeat and commotional group Johnny had seen them be for the last four years, but at least they were talking. He still wanted to be part of that group.

"I finished the ice cream machine," Jerry said. He was now nothing more than a co-worker.

"I'm almost finished," Johnny answered facing the window. His voice bordered on cold even though he didn't mean it.

Jerry looked over his shoulder. "Aren't there usually seven of them?"

"Yeah," Johnny said.

"Cheerleader, right? Where d'you think she went?"

"I don't know," Johnny said. "Did you finish the deposit?"

"Yeah, it's in the safe."

"If you want I can close up," Johnny offered. "Phil gave me a key. All I have to do is mop."

"Sure," Jerry said. "If you don't need any help."

"There's only one mop."

"Fine by me," Jerry said. "See you at school. I'll get the lights outside."

"Thanks," Johnny said.

Jerry left.

Johnny watched the teenagers at the picnic table until the lights went out.

Where did she go? A town this small, no one should be able to disappear without anyone knowing.

The football players escorted the cheerleaders to their cars.

Johnny was alone. He made the mop bucket and did his final chore for the night. He sloshed soapy water on the floor and spread it to each corner. When he was done, he dumped the pail out over the drainage grill in the center of the floor.

He made a shot of root beer. They weren't supposed to sneak drinks on the clock, but he was alone. No reason to abide by every rule, right?

On the way out the door, he flipped the light switch, and locked the door from the inside. He left the building, and put his coat on outside. His bike was locked up on the electricity pole. He walked to it, watching his breath fog the air. He practiced dribbling an imaginary ball around imaginary defenders. When he reached his bike, he shot the game-winning short shot.

Johnny unchained his bike, and climbed on it. He started toward his house.

An engine roared to life. There were no headlights, so he didn't see who it was. He could only hear the motor. The engine revved loudly. Johnny tried to ignore it. It was somewhere ahead of him. It wasn't moving so he assumed it was someone showing off for a girl. He pedaled faster hoping it would get him home quicker.

As he passed Market Street, the white and baby blue Super Clipper spun its tires and lurched forward. Johnny couldn't stop or dodge the grille so the only choice he had was to hit the fender and fall over the hood. Johnny groaned in pain.

"What the hell, little bitch?" Rodney said, slamming the door to the car. "You scratched my car, you pussy."

"What's the problem?" Brett said.

"Do you even know how to ride that thing?" Eli added.

"Please, Rodney," Johnny pleaded. He just wanted to go home and wonder what happened to the seventh person at the picnic table. The cheerleader who stopped coming to Phil's. Johnny rolled off the hood to the ground. "Don't do this."

"Oh, don't want to," Rodney said. "It's a crime scene now. You damaged my car."

"We should call the sheriff, Rodney," Brett heckled.

"Nah, we gonna handle this ourselves," Rodney said. "Put his ass in the trunk."

"Seriously?" Brett said.

"Yeah, I'm fuckin' serious," Rodney screamed. "Who do you think was behind the reason we spent last year in the detention center?"

"How would he know?" Eli asked.

"Because little bitch here was there when we was setting up the nails."

"You could've killed the janitor. There was blood everywhere."

"Was?" Rodney shouted. "I think you mean there will be. I said put him in the trunk."

There was another resistant pause, and then Eli and Brett both moved on Johnny. They yanked him up by his elbows and dragged him to the back of the Clipper. Johnny groaned and mumbled a protest.

Rodney opened the trunk, and his lackeys threw Johnny inside it. Johnny's head hit a brick. He saw stars. The trunk slammed hard enough to rock the car on its axels. Johnny felt around the trunk. There were bricks and large pieces of cinderblocks all around. He even felt a car jack at his feet. The car revved loudly, and Rodney floored the gas pedal. The bricks behind Johnny fell over onto him. They crushed his back. The corners of the brick jammed into his ribs. The car jerked to the side toppling more bricks down on Johnny. The tires shrieked through the night air. The car jack slammed into Johnny's thigh. He shouted in pain. Eli and Brett pounded on the back seat, laughing like maniacs. They accelerated down the street and cut a hard turn into a parking lot. There was a dip, and the stones shifted again.

Rodney slammed on the brakes. More bricks came down on Johnny. One crashed into his temple, and Johnny nearly blacked out.

The tires shrieked again, and the car spun circles, sending the bricks and tools bouncing around the inside of the trunk. The car slammed on brakes again. Johnny heard Rodney's door open and slam. His footsteps travelled down the length of the car.

The memory faded, and Johnny started spinning again. He was laughing with his beautiful wife, and their adopted, stuffed son. The centrifugal force of their spinning eggshell pushed Johnny toward the backrest.

"Faster!" Harriet shouted. She was frantically pulling at the control.

Johnny's hand grew heavy from the force. He couldn't hold onto the spinning mechanism without gripping it with all his strength. He let go of the control, hoping that with only Harriet spinning the eggshell they would slow down, but it didn't. The force pinned his hand to his chest.

"We're going so fast!" Harriet shouted. Her laughter filled the eggshell. Even though they were both laughing, she was obviously having a better time on this ride than Johnny. She continued to spin.

Johnny couldn't lift his head from the metal eggshell. The view outside their pod was too blurry to process. The green and pink lights smeared together like glowing paint. He could hear the people in the other eggshells whooping and hollering. The energy from all around him fed his own cheer, but his worry remained. He closed his eyes. The laughter, the engine, and the uncontrollable force slinging him into oblivion, all shoved him back into the trunk of the Clipper. He couldn't see. He couldn't swat away the bricks. He couldn't protect his face or curl up into a protective ball. All he could do was laugh.

Johnny opened his eyes. He had to get out of the trunk, and get back to his wife. The sight outside the pod horrified him. It was Rodney, Brett, and Eli watching him from in front of the oily green and pink smear. They wore the same dirty jeans and tattered tee shirts they always wore, but their faces were gone. They stared from the empty sockets of their white skulls. In front of him his dad was swinging a shovel like a mallet. It clanged on the metallic platform. Sparks ignited.

"He's coming for you, little bitch," Rodney said.

Merle screamed an angry throat splitting roar.

Johnny screamed. It sounded like terror, but it tapered off into a wild cackle. He closed his eyes.

Harriet put her hand on his leg. The motor underneath the platform decelerated. The force released Johnny, and he was able to move his arms and lift his head from the metal eggshell. His head swam.

"Wasn't that great?" Harriet said.

"It was…" Johnny couldn't finish.

"You dizzy?" Harriet giggled. "I told you you'd be dizzy."

The brakes in the platform screeched.

The eggshells slowly stopped spinning, and the bar lifted from their lap. Harriet picked Griz up from the seat beside her and nudged Johnny to slide out. He stepped off the ride. His legs were weak, and he almost fell. Harriet held his arm to stabilize him. She helped him walk off the platform.

"A little dizzy?" Larry said, holding the exit door open for them.

"And we just ate," Harriet said.

"I think I'm fine. Just dizzy."

"As long as it was fun," Larry said. Then it seemed like he made a point to just ask Harriet, "Where to next?"

"Haunted house," she answered.

Larry's face lit up. "Is that right?"

"Yeah," Johnny answered weakly.

"Careful. It's scary. And they's wild animals afoot."

6
Haunted House

Johnny's head swam. He hadn't been this lightheaded since the sheriff had told him that his mother had died. Little Johnny was only six, and he wasn't able to fully understand that he'd never see her again. He sat on his bed all night in a haze of confusion. His dad didn't come home for two days. He wandered around the neighborhood looking for them.

"Have you seen my mom?" Little Johnny asked Little Jerry. His breath fogged between them.

"No," Jerry answered. "I'll ask my mom to help us find her. She's not home yet though. I can help you look for her."

"I don't know where she is," Johnny began to cry again.

"Do you want to play tricks with me?"

"No," Johnny said.

"I'm Jerry."

"I'm Jonathan. My mom calls me Johnny."

"Do you want me to help you look for her?"

"Yeah."

"Let's go find her."

They searched the neighborhood for hours. They didn't find her. It wasn't until Jerry's mother came home that there was any sort of closure on the matter. She told him the truth about what happened to his mother, about the car crash. Johnny and Jerry's mother had a long talk about heaven and that his mother was up there with his old dog that got run over by daddy's truck. She told him that the two of them were waiting for him and watching him to make sure nothing bad ever happened to him. Johnny cried, because he would never get to see her alive again. But he was happy that he would see her in heaven.

Jerry's mother walked him home and made macaroni and cheese for him. She stayed there until dark, then she left to make Jerry and his sister and dad supper.

That night Merle got home. He sloshed through the house to his bed. The springs strained under his weight.

Johnny smelled the whiskey from his bedroom. He didn't feel any better about his mother, and he cried himself to sleep. It was the worst day of his life. He stayed in a weird haze of pain and loss that his mind didn't have the capacity to decipher. The thing about pain is that eventually it becomes normal. People forget the pain is there.

As that lightheaded feeling left, Johnny became more aware that he was being pulled down the midway. His heart started pounding as his mind put together everything since he left the reunion.

The rides. The rides are...they're not right.

"Come on," Harriet said. "We're almost there."

"Stop," Johnny said weakly. "Hang on."

"No, come on. It's right there."

"No." Johnny struggled to connect the pieces. "How'd you get in my car?"

"What do you mean, honey?"

"My car," Johnny said. "I was alone, and then you were there. I was mad, and you showed up. You made it better. Where were you?"

Harriet sighed. "I was always there. We've been together since high school."

"But we weren't. We never talked. You weren't there our senior year. You disappeared."

"That's not—"

"I remember," Johnny said. His voice was fast, and the words were starting to run into each other on the way out. "That night Rodney got out from the detention center. You weren't there with the other cheerleaders. They came after the football playoffs. They were there, and you had been missing. No one even seemed to notice but me."

"Honey, calm down."

"Now, you're here? What is this place?"

"It's a carnival."

"Where've you been this whole time? Are we even married?"

Harriet changed then. Her voice lowered, and her hands took on a more natural state for her. Griz dropped to the ground. Instead of skin, her hands were shrouded in a black fog. She raised them to his head. "You need to calm down."

She placed her thumb on his forehead between his eyes. Her other hand braced his head.

Johnny went cold. His eyes turned black, and his head jerked backward as if he was screaming at the sky. His lungs emptied, and he gasped for air. Slowly, his heart rate calmed.

Harriet's eyes filled. She pulled him to her in a gentle embrace. "I'm sorry," she whispered into his ear. "I know it hurts, but it'll get better. I'm here. I'll be here forever. I love you, Johnny."

"I love you," Johnny said.

"Do you feel better?"

"Yes," Johnny said. It was as though nothing was ever wrong.

"So what do you say?" Harriet grinned. "Let's go to the haunted house?"

"Please," Johnny said. He was relieved to be staying on the ground. "After that last ride, my stomach needs a break."

"Well, let's go," Harriet said.

Harriet turned, and behind her was the large mansion with the cracked black paint. The windows and door was a horrified face. Aside from that, it could've been any other house in the country. She walked toward the house, and Johnny followed. Of course he did. He would've followed her anywhere. I can still hear his loafers *crunch crunch crunch* down the midway toward the house.

There was a sign on the door engraved in a black metal

plate that said: Leave now or encounter The Horrors of Rose Colline.

"See," Harriet said, giddy as you please. "Scary, right?"

"Yeah," Johnny agreed, looking uneasy at the black sign screwed into the door. He wondered if Harriet saw the drops of red streaking down the wood.

"There's no line," Harriet pointed out. "There's never a line. People don't usually go back in once they come out."

"I can imagine." Johnny pushed the door open.

A recording of my voice played through the horn of the old record player just inside. It sat on an old table next to an oil lamp. The table waited just inside the entrance. Across from it, an opening in the wall stood, dark and cold. There were thick black curtains hiding what lay just beyond its threshold. On either side of the opening there is a six-foot tall statue of a hissing green cobra. The fangs dripped black liquid. The eyes were glowing yellow.

"Welcome," the recording said. "This building is home to some of the most evil and horrifying things ever to haunt mankind. You may turn back should you wish to keep your soul. For the rest of you, the brave, step through the curtain and discover the horrors of Rose Colline." That's when the air flows through the curtains, so it looks like they are reaching for you. All part of the show.

You see, friend, The Horrors of Rose Colline is different from the rest of the haunted houses around the world, because, you see, the house at Dandy D's Carnival Funland is actually haunted. Sure, some of the effects on the walls of the hallways in The Horrors of Rose Colline are manmade, absolutely. I would never hide behind that, but it is haunted. Not by demons or ghosts exactly, but haunted just the same.

Harriet walked up to the statues. She prodded one with her finger. "See, it looks pretty scary."

"No doubt," Johnny said. "Really spooky."

"Come on!" Harriet bolted through the curtains, laughing like a child.

"Wait," Johnny said. She was already gone. Johnny watched the statue suspiciously. Something held him there for a moment. He felt like he was being hypnotized. He never believed in that sort of thing, so he shook the feeling away.

"Come on, Johnny!" Harriet said from somewhere deep in the house.

Geez, how far did she go?

"Wait for me!" Johnny called back to her.

He pushed past the curtains. Just beyond them, there was a long corridor. The only light came from a black bulb at the end of the hall. It illuminated the paint on the walls. Johnny glanced around unimpressed as he made his way through the house. The paintings were cartoonish drawings of classic scary images. Vampires, mummies, swamp creatures, werewolves, and beneath the bulb at the end of the hall was a depiction of me wearing a cloak of shadows, holding a scythe with boney fingers. Something about the blade made Johnny reach out to touch the wall, but he was interrupted.

Harriet's voice called to him from behind a door around the corner.

Johnny cautiously turned his attention to her voice. He

pushed the door open. Simulated lightning and wind welcomed him into the next room. Fake trees and papier-mâché tombstones created a path through a grassy field to the entrance to a bell tower. A nagging twinge of panic started to grow deep in Johnny's mind. He would've turned back and waited for Harriet to come out, but her voice lured him deeper into the house. He walked into the bell tower, and the wooden door banged closed, locking him inside a dark, cool corridor. The room was made of stone, and he used his fingers to navigate the interior. His hands nervously shook. A square gap in the wall just overhead showed an image of a manmade rainstorm, while pain-filled groans came to him through the stone.

"Harriet?" Johnny's voice cracked.

The stone wall ended, and he could see dull light down a long tunnel. Johnny hurried his pace, ignoring the bursts of wind and mist as he jogged toward the light. The midway came into view just as Johnny struck the glass. Harriet waited on the midway pointing to the opposite end of the house. The gash was back on her face. He watched Harriet waste away into a thin layer of tightly stretched skin over a boney skeleton. The wound on her face peeled back showing most of the skull on the right side. Up and down her arms and on her neck, there were thin cuts. Seeing her that way filled Johnny with fire.

Then he saw what happened to her. It played in front of him like one of those television pictures. It was almost like he was in the room with them. There were bunk beds along all the walls of a wooden cabin. There were other girls laughing. Not like the laughter at Dandy D's, no. No, laughter like that meant that someone was at the butt of some kind of joke. Laughter like that meant someone was hurt. There were girls throwing empty Coke bottles at a closet door. Someone screamed and pounded on the other side. Johnny looked at each face and realized that none of them was Harriet. The voice coming from the closet suddenly became familiar.

"Please," Harriet screamed. "Let me out. I'm not supposed to be in closed spaces like this."

"We know," one of the girls said. Johnny recognized her from the picnic bench outside of Phil's. Her name was Amy Shoemaker. "Jenny hadn't never seen someone pitch a fit before. We want to see if it's true."

"No, please!" Harriet pleaded. She pounded on the door working herself up to the very thing she was trying to avoid.

"Just do it already," another girl said. Johnny had never seen her before.

"Let's put a snake in there with her," another said. Johnny recognized her from the bench, too. He couldn't remember her name though.

"Better hurry," Amy shouted. "Carrie's getting a snake."

Harriet screamed louder. Her fists on the door drummed wildly. "Let me out! L—Let me…" She trailed off and there was a thump against the door.

"She's doing it!" Amy said, laughing. "Open the door."

The girl Johnny didn't recognize unlocked the door. It flung open. Harriet fell into the glass. Her hands twitched as she jerked around on the floor. Her mouth lolled open, and her eyes looked like they were staring into another world.

"Oh, shit," Carrie said.

"Look at her!" Amy shouted. Johnny wanted to slam her against a wall by her feet, but the glass stopped him from taking another step.

Harriet twitched on the floor, with the other girls pointing, laughing, and busting more bottles on the floor. Her twitching slowly became tremors. The faraway look in her eyes was replaced by embarrassment and pain. All around her was pain. Her arms, her neck, her legs, all were covered in cuts. And rather than a soothing voice to bring her back from the seizure, there was laughing. She crawled through the glass, and climbed to her feet. She wouldn't let them see her cry. Like a newborn calf, she stumbled out of the cabin to her mother's car. Johnny watched them for a moment, fit to puke. He turned away from the glass. He sat on a nearby stone. He rubbed the anger from his eyes.

Then Johnny was in the car with her. She was crying. Her clothes were torn in multiple places. Her socks lay on the car between them. There were red spots all over them. There were pieces of glass bottle in her hair. Harriet shoved peppermint after peppermint into her mouth.

"I didn't even want to go," she said. But she wasn't talking directly to him. It was as though he was watching a scene from a movie that had later been dubbed over with a new voice. She spoke through her hands, which covered her face. "My parents were going on vacation. I asked to go with them, but they said they didn't have enough money for three people to go. I told them I could take care of myself for a week in the house. They didn't listen. What they wanted was a week away from me. They didn't even go out of town."

"Harriet," Johnny said. His voice cracked. He reached for her, but he couldn't touch her. Deep down he knew he wouldn't be able to anyway.

Harriet yelled in frustration. She took the keys from her pocket and started the car. She backed away from the cabin slowly and wiped the blood from her face. She pulled back onto the Five and headed back to Nowheresville. "This was my first time in Rose Colline. They were my friends. Amy's dad had a cabin there where he always stayed when he went hunting. I didn't want to go. I never felt like I was part of their group. Or any group for that matter."

The car accelerated.

Ahead there was a sign for a Dandy D's Carnival Funland. It was nearly midnight, so she watched the sign and wondered what it'd be like to go there with no one else around. To be the only person in the entire carnival.

Johnny saw the truck pull out in front of her. It carried long metal pipes in the bed. They jutted out like a tail.

"Harriet, watch out," Johnny said.

The seventeen year-old Harriet wasn't listening. She stared at the billboard. The colors were so bright.

The truck in front of them didn't speed up or get out of the way.

"Harriet, the truck," Johnny said. "The truck!"

Harriet read the sign, "Dandy D's Carnival Fun—"

Harriet's car crashed into the back of the truck. The metal

pipes came through the windshield.

Johnny listened to the crash, and covered his eyes. When nothing happened he opened them again. He was back in the haunted house.

"It's about pain, Johnny," I told him. He wasn't to me yet, but I knew that if I didn't say anything, he would never have gotten off the stone. "You have to keep going."

Johnny stood from the stone. "Who are you?"

"Come and see," I told him. "I've been waiting."

The glass faded away. Johnny held his hand up to where the glass had been, but nothing stopped his fingers. He continued through the tunnel. There was the sound of a car's tires screeching. Even though he knew what car it was, he kept walking. Only a few feet ahead there was another glass wall. He held his hands up, so he wouldn't run into it. The baby blue and white Super Clipper spun circles in the Phil's Drive-Thru parking lot. The brick tumbled around in the trunk. The car came to an abrupt stop. Rodney got out with the keys in his hand. He opened the trunk and dragged Johnny out of it.

Johnny saw himself. He was bloody, and his face was swollen.

"You took a year from me, little bitch," Rodney said. He kicked him hard.

I don't remember this. Johnny thought. *I thought they just left me there.*

"Take his shit," Rodney said.

Brett and Eli got out of the car then. They went through Johnny's pockets. The only things they found were a key to the bike lock and his wallet. Inside there was three dollars, which Rodney pocketed, a library card, which made its way to the ground, and a picture of Johnny's mother.

"Is that your dead mom?" Brett asked. It wasn't a question he wanted to have answered. It was a taunt.

"She's perty," Eli mocked.

"Let me see that," Rodney said. He snatched the picture of Edie from Brett's hand. "Oh, she *is* perty. Pick him up."

Brett and Eli picked Johnny off the ground and held him up by his arms. They expected Rodney to come down on him. They gave him room to swing, but that didn't happen.

"You think your dad knew what to do with this kind of woman, little bitch?"

Johnny groaned. His mouth was bleeding. "Give it back."

"You gonna get it back," Rodney said. He unzipped his pants, and spit in his free hand. "I bet she was good. Too bad she ain't here no more."

Brett and Eli grimaced, but they kept quiet. Brett turned his head while Rodney stroked himself, but Eli didn't.

"Better watch," Eli said. He yanked Johnny's head up by his hair.

Johnny watched this from behind the glass. His stomach turned over, and he vomited soda and corndog on the floor. It took too long. Every time he wiped his mouth, he would see Rodney still standing there in the parking lot with his mother's picture in his hand, and his stomach would flip again.

When it was finally over, Rodney threw the picture on

the ground and spit. He zipped his pants, and lit a cigarette. "Thanks, little bitch. That was fun. You can let him go."

Brett slugged Johnny in the gut. The air escaped him, and Johnny hit the ground. Everything went black.

Even the glass wall.

Johnny fell to his knees, sobbing loudly. His stomach hitched, but there was nothing left to send. After a long moment, Johnny stood again.

"What is this?"

I said nothing.

"*Huh?*" Johnny shouted. "Pain? Torture? Why are you showing me this? That was ten years ago. I'm over that."

"But you're not," I said.

The glass faded, opening the tunnel again. There was a wind at his back pushing him forward. Johnny walked through the tunnel. There was no light. He felt his way through the tunnel with one hand on the stone wall, and the other in front of him. There was the occasional drip from the ceiling onto the floor but nothing else.

He was scared. They're always scared if they've made it this far.

"What do you want?" he said.

A familiar sound emanated from deep down the tunnel. A buzz grew from up ahead. It wasn't the buzzer that controlled time at basketball games. It was the sound of cicadas. It crescendoed to a decibel so loud that Johnny could feel the vibrations in the wall.

rrrrEEEEEEEE EEE EEE EEEEEEEE

Ahead of him, a pair of green eyes opened. That hacking

cough echoed through the tunnel. The cicadas continued their howl.

rrrrEEEEEEEE EEE EEE EEEEEEEE

Johnny stopped. The thing from the woods was here in front of him. It watched him again. The hacking cough turned to a laugh again. The cicadas broke into an insectile laugh with it. Then children, from all around him, joined the thing in the tunnel.

Johnny tried to stop himself, but the chuckle inside him turned to a giggle. It escalated to a mad cackle. He fell to the floor struggling to breathe. He turned on his stomach and raised himself to crawl. He inched toward the thing that watched him with those glowing green eyes.

The thing charged him. Johnny heard the beating feet on the floor. He could feel it coming closer. The cicadas roared all around him. Johnny met them with hysterical laughter.

The thing stampeded toward Johnny, and just as it reached him, the eyes blinked out. The air of its momentum washed over his face. The tunnel fell silent with the exception of Johnny's cackle. Slowly, he began to scream.

"*What do you want?*" Johnny shrieked.

"I want to give you purpose," I said. I stood above him, looking down at his broken soul. "All your life, you've been nothing to no one. You've dealt with this pain all your life, but you never got past it. Rodney nearly beat you to the end of your life for four years. You never got to be Harriet's one and only. That tore you apart. That's something you can have now. You two were just alike. No one could be bothered to humor either of y'all. You were made to be together.

You were made to be here."

"Here?" Johnny said. "At the carnival."

"Yes," I said. "There are lives for everyone. In the lives y'all lived, they was only pain. Pain of loss. Fear. The pain of never being good enough. Life ain't worth keepin' if you only have that to look forward to. If that's all your life is, how can you even hope to be happy? You see, Johnny, I think pain is the feeling you have when some part of you, something you love, is dying. I'm gone take that from you. And I'm going to give you everything you want."

Johnny saw his mother behind me. She glowed. She always did that in Johnny's eyes. She wore the same dress she did the first time they had come to Dandy D's. Her hair fell behind her in waves. She was smiling at him. Finally, Johnny collected enough strength to stand. He walked past me to her.

"Johnny," she said softly.

It was the first time he heard her voice in twenty years. Tears poured out of him. He reached for her, and to his surprise, he felt her there. He embraced her.

"I'm proud of you, Johnny," she said. And then she was gone.

"You'll always be able to see her," I told him. "If you stay. But you need to know the truth."

In front of them, a final glass wall played a scene.

Merle and Edie were at a year-end party for the workers at the plant. It was New Year's Eve. The company had just renewed the contract to continue producing tanks for the war efforts. Only this time, the plant was built just outside nearby Rose Colline. No more weeklong work shifts. No more driving hours to work. Just hop in the car, and twenty minutes later, he'd be clocking in for the day. Merle brought her with him, not because family was invited, or because he wanted her to be there to celebrate. Edie insisted she come, because alcohol would be there. Merle was one to imbibe in the excessive lifestyle.

The sun hadn't fully snuck below the horizon when Merle stumbled out of the newly christened plant with Edie to hold him up.

"I think I should probably drive us home," she said. She had stopped at the driver's side door of the old Ford.

"What?" Merle said. "You ain't got no damn license."

"That doesn't mean I can't do it."

"Just get in. I'm fine," Merle said.

"You're falling all over yourself, Merle," Edie said. She was pleading now. "Our son is at home. By himself."

"Well, maybe we should stay. Give your tits a break."

"Fine," Edie said. "If you're going to make a fool of yourself in front of God and everybody, let's go."

Edie got in the car and slid over enough for him to sit beside her. She wanted to at least be able to reach the wheel. Merle pushed her to the passenger seat. There were no seatbelts in the car, so she gripped the armrest on the door. He took the revolver out of the waist band of his jeans and sat it on the seat between them. He started the car and put it in gear. It jerked forward before stalling. He cursed the engine and turned the ignition again. His inebriated brain managed to get the car back on the road. He slalomed back and forth between lanes. The tire slid off the shoulder of the road, and he jerked the wheel hard to get the car back on the road.

"This thing ain't driving right," he said too loudly. "Remind me to look at it in the morning."

"I don't think it's the car," Edie said.

"What'd you say?"

"I said I think you're drunk," she amended. "That's why it's not driving right."

Merle looked at her. He slapped her hard enough to swivel her head. "First you make our boy a queer, and then you're going to try to run me?"

"You are drunk," Edie said with her forehead resting on the cold window. She stared at the glowing pink hill on the other side. She imagined pushing little Johnny on a swing dangling from the oak tree. She put her fingers on the door handle when he swerved again.

"I'm as drunk as you are stupid," Merle said. He slapped her again. "Come here."

"No," Edie said. The car jerked back into their lane. There was another car on the road then. "Someone's coming."

"You don't think I see the goddamn car, Edie?" Merle yelled. He grabbed the gun and swung the butt of it at her face.

Edie's cheek took the brunt of the blow, and she fell back against the window. He had never done more than slap her before. The shock took her breath away. Her free hand touched the swollen cheek. She watched the headlights coming toward them. "You hit me," she said.

"You said I was drunk," Merle replied.

"You hit me," she repeated.

"I heard you the first time."

The tire fell off the shoulder again. Merle jerked the wheel, over correcting. He accidently squeezed the trigger of the gun, firing into the windshield. The bullet caused the glass to spiderweb. The car ahead of them honked.

Merle jerked the wheel again. Edie's hand involuntarily pulled the door handle. The car coming toward them clipped the back bumper, sending Merle and Edie spinning into a ditch. The door flung open. Edie fell halfway out of the car as it began to roll. Merle was flung into the windshield and blacked out.

When the Ford came to a stop, it had left Edie's broken, lifeless body in the ditch thirty feet away. Merle lay with everything above the waist hanging out of the opening where the windshield had been. Nobody was injured from the oncoming car. He was a mechanic so he was able to fix the smashed bumper himself. Given the situation, it was the least he could do. Merle stayed in the hospital for two days. Edie stayed in the ground forever.

"You have a choice, Johnny," I said. "You can leave, but it ain't gone get better. Or you can stay here. With us. You'll bring happiness to everyone. But you need closure either way."

"Where is he?" Johnny said through gritting teeth.

The glass changed from the flotsam and carnage from all those years ago to the living room of his old home. His dad was staring off into space in a rocking chair. He had a beer in one hand, and the revolver in the other.

Johnny watched as the glass vanished. He stepped into the living room.

"Well, look who it is," Merle said. "Where you been ten years?"

"You killed my mother?"

"Are you kidding me?" Merle barked a laugh. "Twenty years, and still ain't off that tit a'hers. Maybe I did. What you gone do about it?"

Johnny didn't move except for the trembling rage in his muscles.

"I tell you what boy. You wanna do something about her," He tossed the gun to Johnny. "They's only one way to use—"

Johnny pulled the trigger.

The gun clicked, banishing all sound from the house. He pulled it again. Nothing happened. He stared at the gun, bewildered.

"I'll be goddamned," Merle said.

Johnny pulled the trigger one last time.

Merle laughed the way people laugh when someone is being hurt. "Maybe there is something in that little beanbag a'yours, boy. Put that thing down. You earned a beer."

Merle reached under his chair. He tossed Johnny a can. It hit the floor and busted open. The smell of beer filled the room.

"You ruined a beer," Merle said. "You fu—"

Johnny stormed ahead. Merle didn't move. He didn't expect Johnny to come down on him. Johnny raised the gun and struck Merle between the eyes. He saw stars.

Johnny screamed as the gun came down again. Over and over. Blood splashed on the white button-up shirt that Johnny wore. He hammered until what he was hitting didn't feel like a skull anymore.

When Merle was finished, Johnny picked the teeth and splinters of bone out of his hand. He stood above his prey like a wolf. His animal instinct exploded from his mouth, expelling the grief and allowing closure to fill him like cool water. Johnny was unburdened now by the always-watching eye of the small town where he began his life. He laughed at the stains on the wall and the one spreading across the floor. Johnny changed then. His eyes went black. His arms took on a consistency more like ours. They faded in the dim living room. Fog took their place, a thick black fog. The revolver thumped onto the ground.

He didn't see me behind him, but he knew I was there.

"Welcome to Johnny D's Carnival Funland," I said.

"Welcome to the family, Johnny," Harriet said. She slid her fingers between his, and held Griz like a toddler on her hip. "I'm so happy you're here."

7

Johnny D's Carnival Funland

That's it, friend. That's how I got my guy. Johnny D's Carnival Funland has thrived ever since. The kids love him. Parents love him even more. We even built a stage, a pedestal really. We raised him six feet above the ground and gave him a car. They's just something I want to assure you before we get where we're going. I help the people I take deal with the pain of their pasts. I help them get to a better place so they don't hurt when they leave. You remember me tellin' ya Harriet left the table after eating her dog and soda? There's more to that part of the story than a simple restroom break.

You see, when she took off, she met up with an old friend.

Did I tell you that Rodney Malone smoked home-rolled cigarettes?

It started back in high school. He stole them from his

dad's Tender Box stash. When he and his wife got in his car after the reunion, he lit up a rolled cigarette, one he rolled from the Tender Box tin that he bought himself. His wife was drunk, and when she got that way, she infuriated Rodney.

"Would you just get in the car? Jesus Christ." Rodney took a drag from the cigarette.

"I'm coming," his wife said.

"Shut the door," Rodney said. The car he drove in high school was working a lot better than the 1950 Dodge Dart that Johnny had. Rodney mainly kept it in the garage in favor of his work truck. The door shut, and the engine rumbled to life.

"I think I'm going to be sick."

"You better fuckin' not," Rodney said. He pulled a bag of nails out from underneath the seat. "Here. If you're going to puke do it in this. Get in the back and lay down."

His wife fell over the seat and dropped onto the back bench.

"Careful," Rodney scolded. "It's not a goddamn trampoline."

The Clipper spun its tires as it left the parking lot.

"What the hell," she cried from the back seat.

"Shut up," Rodney said. "It's your own fault you're sick. You ain't had to drink everything in there."

"You're an asshole."

"Yeah, well we getting home, ain't we? No fuckin' thanks to you. Why the hell cain't you control yourself in public? You make me look stupid."

"You two don't fight," a voice smooth like jazz said from the passenger side of the Clipper. She wasn't fully there. She was a smoky skeleton of herself. Rather than a dress, she wore a black fog into which her body faded.

"Who the hell is she, Rodney?"

"Have you ever ridden a tilt-a-whirl, Rodney?" Harriet said. "The trick is to spin it as hard as you can." Harriet reached toward Rodney. Her smoky limb entered his mouth. She reached into him. He bled from his ears. His hands left the steering wheel to cover his eyes before they were jettisoned out of his head. Harriet reached with the other arm to grip the wheel. "Goodbye, Rodney," she said and jerked the wheel, sending the car into the trees lining the road.

When the sheriff found Rodney and his wife, they had to peel him out of the overturned car. She was shrieking even after she crawled from the debris and flotsam. They sent her up to Mississippi to Whitfield for screaming about ghosts attacking the car.

That's not what you get at Johnny D's Carnival Funland though. The only thing you can expect is fun. Nothing but entertainment, food, and happy families. You will never go home unhappy. That's what we're selling. Happiness. And it starts right at the beginning. With the barker. With Johnny D.

You can hear his boisterous voice from the gravel parking lot. He's on the stage standing in front of a 1949 white and baby blue Super Clipper. Rebuilt, of course.

"Come fun, come all!" The barker hollers with fervor, making wide, sweeping gestures with his arms. "Eat the delicious dogs and cotton candy! Grab a soda! Games for the entire family! See the sights! Ride the rides! Brothers and sisters!"

"Mamas and papas!" A voice smooth like jazz joins him from the woman in the black dress with the sparkles like every star in the galaxy is woven right into the fabric. Her white smile glows in the fading sunlight. Her lips are as pink as the hill that gave our town its name.

"Players and cheerleaders!" They join hands then. Great showmanship. Beautiful people. "There's something for all of you here at Johnny D's Carnival Funland! You there, the happy couple! Yes, you two! I can't in good faith charge a couple of lovers as happy as you! Come on in!"

"But be careful," she says.

"That's right," he adds. "They's wild animals afoot."

It's amazing to watch. I know everything we put together is in good hands when I hear those two.

But you're here for business. You want to open a theater. Did I ever tell you what I wanted to put in the open space next to my haunted house?

I didn't?

Walk with me, friend.

Let's talk business.

Under the Wolf Tree

Continues in...

The Nelson House

It's hurricane season. Johnny D's Carnival Funland is closing early for the night as Rose Colline braces for the storm of the decade. Kevin Maxey and his friends are going to do it. They're spending the night in the Nelson House. As the town hunkers down beneath the heavy clouds, Kevin and his friends break into Rose Colline's real haunted house and wait for the storm. Spending the night in the Nelson House is all Kevin needs to jettison himself to the top of their small town popularity, but the hurricane isn't the only thing coming for them.

Kevin will have to face an evil terror when the lights go out. The storm threatens to destroy the house around him, but the horrors don't end when the skies are clear...

For more details and information,
visit www.SilverLeafBooks.com

ABOUT THE AUTHOR

Josh Stricklin is an American author and musician with degrees in English literature and advertising from the University of Southern Mississippi. *Ridin' the 5* is his second terrifying novel with Silver Leaf Books. He's currently hard at work continuing his first series.